To Guy

Wrong Place, Wrong Time

Alan Rice

Best Wishes

Alan Rice

Pen Press Publishers Ltd

First published in Great Britain by
Pen Press Publishers Ltd
25 Eastern Place
Brighton
BN2 1GJ

ISBN13: 978-906206-67-3

Printed and bound in the UK

A catalogue record of this book is available from
the British Library

Cover design by Jacqueline Abromeit

For my lovely wife Mo, without whose support and encouragement this would never have been written let alone published.

&

To the memory of my Mother and Father, Rene and Charlie, who will always be in my heart.

About the Author

Alan Rice is 55 years young and lives with his wife Mo in the historic town of Berkhamsted, Hertfordshire.

Born in Fulham, London, his family moved to Hemel Hempstead when he was only four years old and, surprisingly, took him along. Apart from three years shared between St Ives, Cambridgeshire and Daventry, Northamptonshire, he has always lived in or around "Hemel" or "Berko".

His claims to fame are that he has played guitar and sang in a pub-rock band and actually got paid for it and has ridden a Harley Davidson out into the Navada desert without falling off once.

In between writing he earns a crust working "in computers", a phrase that no longer draws the admiring glances that it did twenty-odd years ago when he first uttered it.

He has two children: Nikki and Dean, two stepchildren: Helen and Kate, and four grandchildren: Rachel, Christopher, Erin and Gracie all of whom keep him young and insane.

Chapter 1

The blue and white striped tape fluttered in the early morning breeze. Stretched across the entrance to the park, it was patrolled by a lone police constable in a Day-Glo yellow vest wielding a clipboard. Beyond it, police vehicles were parked at random churning huge swathes out of the carefully laid turf and white-suited police officers were either searching the ground in microscopic detail or striding purposefully on some errand. The whole scene was made surreal by the complete lack of sound; only the rustling of the trees and morning birdsong could be heard.

At the heart of this activity a white tent had been erected to contain the immediate crime scene. Inspector Greenwold and Sergeant Cotteril – also clad in white – stood looking solemnly at the victim. The inspector was unshaven and his bloodshot eyes gave testament to the early hour. His companion swayed gently alongside him as if in sympathy with the breeze. The Sergeant's face showed the rigours of having been on the town all night; he had only just fallen into bed when the call came through.

The deceased was a middle-aged man lying on his front with his head turned to the right. His eyes and mouth were wide in surprise or shock and the right arm outstretched as if grasping at something or someone. The other arm was tucked under his body raising his chest off the ground.

What they could see of his clothes suggested money. A three quarter length leather coat and Italian shoes were all that were on view but even these two items exceeded Inspector Greenwold's annual clothing budget.

"Finished, sir," the photographer said as he stood aside awaiting further instruction. The forensic pathologist, Colin, advanced on the body and crouched down.

"How long do you think?" The inspector asked.

Colin looked up with a "give me a chance" expression, and then continued with his examination. A few moments later he said, "Last night sometime, possibly near midnight is the best I can do for the moment."

Sergeant Cotteril duly made a note of it, not that he thought they would forget. The action was more to give him something to do, something to focus his pounding brain on. Also, the way he felt he really did not want to get any closer, there was sure to be a lot of "claret" around and his churning stomach would certainly rebel.

"Any ID?" the inspector asked hopefully as Colin fished a wallet out of the man's coat pocket.

"A Mr Brian Prentice," he answered, "of 23, The Willows, Perry Green."

Cotteril made a note of this as well as Colin bagged the wallet.

"We'll turn him over now." With the aid of his assistant, the body was rolled onto its back.

Sergeant Cotteril choked back the bile that rose suddenly in his throat; the front of the man was smothered in blood, the cause of which was plain to see. The hilt of a knife protruded from his chest.

Inspector Greenwold whispered, "Saints preserve us."

The path on which the man had been lying was also covered in congealed blood from his neck to part way down his legs.

"He's bled out, as our American friends are fond of calling it," Colin informed them. "I would estimate the knife punctured a major artery, but will confirm it back at the mortuary." The weapon was duly removed, bagged and tagged, but not before he had held it up for the officers to see. "Looks very ordinary, a kitchen knife of some description." Colin stood, his hands on his hips, looking down at the body. "Yes," he said as if reaching some internal agreement, "around midnight I would say." He looked over to the inspector. "Not much else to tell you I'm afraid, Joe. But I may have more once I have him on the table."

"Thank you." He looked up from the body. "Come on, Sergeant, you look as if you could do with some fresh air."

The two men stepped out of the tent, squinting in the sunlight and, as if at some hidden signal, both took a long, deep breath.

The inspector turned to his colleague. "My God, your face is actually green.

"Let's get out of these romper suits and pay 23, The Willows a visit, shall we? Let's see if they've missed him yet."

They struggled out of the white suits. The inspector's tie was crooked, his waistcoat buttoned up wrong and one shoelace hung loose. Sergeant Cotteril looked as if he had got dressed in the dark, in someone else's room. You couldn't really say he was wearing his clothes; they just roughly inhabited the same space.

"I think you had best get home and smartened up first," Inspector Greenwold decided. "And have a gallon of coffee while you're at it. Black. You can pick me up from the station in an hour."

"Yes sir."

As they climbed into their respective cars, Greenwold wound down his window and called across to the sergeant. "Should I ask the nice constable to breathalyse you, Sergeant?"

"Not unless you want to do this one on your own," he answered sullenly and drove away.

Chapter 2

The Willows was in an up-and-coming part of town. Sergeant Cotteril's car tyres scrunched to a halt on the stone-chipped driveway in front of the house. As they disembarked the inspector looked up and said, "You smell that?"

Cotteril didn't risk it, Greenwold could play cruel tricks when he wanted to and no doubt there would be some foul odour that would turn his stomach. "No, sir," he answered truthfully.

"Money," he said, letting his breath out noisily, "lots of it."

A patrol car driven by WPC Cane pulled up behind them and she joined the men as they took in the surroundings.

Number 23 was a different design to that of its neighbours and had the appearance of a doll's house, with a central porch and large, lead-lighted windows to each side. The driveway, flanked by small shrubs, continued on to "his and hers" garages built in the same style and brickwork as the house before exiting onto the road again. A Mercedes sports car was in front of the nearest garage door, crouched as if being held by some invisible leash. It gave the appearance of moving very fast while actually standing still.

There was a bell-pull – nothing as common as a button here – that the sergeant tugged on. He was rewarded by a ringing sound deep in the heart of the house that was clearly made by a bell swinging to and fro. The two men took to looking around, shuffling their feet and thrusting their hands deep in their pockets as they waited. WPC Cane stood patiently behind them.

After what he considered a respectable pause, Inspector Greenwold nodded to the bell-pull and the sergeant tugged it again. This time they could hear movement behind the door and involuntarily stepped back as they heard bolts being savagely pulled and various locks and chains being disengaged.

Finally the door opened to reveal a woman in her forties in a hastily pulled on housecoat and dishevelled hair.

"Yes? What bloody time do you call this?"

"Sorry to call on you so early, madam." Inspector Greenwold realised it must only be just after seven in the morning; the call had come in before daybreak. "Are you Mrs Prentice? Mrs Brian Prentice?"

"Yes, why?"

"I am Inspector Greenwold of Perry Green CID and this is Detective Sergeant Cotteril and WPC Cane. May we come in?"

She looked at the inspector's warrant card and then to the WPC, a feeling of foreboding creeping over her as she stood aside to let them pass.

They moved down the hallway to a kitchen that was dominated by a huge farmhouse table. Matching cupboards and work-surfaces clung to each of the walls. There was no sign of a washing machine, freezer, fridge or dishwasher. The inspector correctly surmised they were hiding behind some of the doors or consigned to a utility room elsewhere. Sergeant Cotteril whistled appreciatively, you could have fit the whole of his flat into this one room.

"What's the little sod done now?" She leant back against the sink and extracted a packet of cigarettes and a lighter from her pockets. "You can lock him up this time, I'm not bailing him out again." She looked nervously at the WPC, something wasn't right. Why was she here?

"I'm sorry madam, we seem to have got off on the wrong foot," the inspector interjected. She took the cigarette from her mouth and instinctively moved to the table and sat on one of the chairs. There was bad news coming.

"Do you know the whereabouts of your husband?"

"Well, I thought … I thought he was upstairs asleep." She half stood, as if to go to see, but something in the inspector's manner stopped her and she slumped back into the chair. "He's not, is he?"

Shaking his head, the inspector continued as gently as he could. "A body was discovered in the park this morning and we have reason to believe that it may be your husband."

"Oh my God!" she gasped. "He's dead? You think my Brian's dead?" She covered her mouth with the back of her hand. "No!" She suddenly stood and ran out of the kitchen with WPC Cane in hot pursuit. They heard her pounding up the stairs, calling out: "Brian? Brian? Are you in there? Brian, answer me!"

A few moments later the WPC helped her down the stairs. "His bed, it hasn't been slept in," she said, ashen faced. "No, it can't be. There must be some mistake. No, not Brian." Her voice was hardly more than a whisper.

WPC Cane, speaking calming words, guided her into the lounge and sat her on the couch.

"I'm sorry but I have to ask you some questions," Greenwold said, not sure she was listening.

Then, just on the edge of hearing: "You're sure it's him?"

"I am afraid so. But we will still need a formal identification... Is there someone else who could…?"

"No, no…" She shook her head. "I'll do it. I'll be all right." She looked up and gave a brave smile. "What happened? How did he…? Was it a heart attack?"

"I'm afraid not. He had been stabbed. Died instantly," he lied. "He wouldn't have felt a thing."

She absorbed the information, struggling to hold on to the words that seemed to float around her. Was she really awake? Was this some kind of nightmare? It felt real, but aren't they supposed to? All sorts of thoughts were clamouring for attention. She shook her head again. "When do you want me to…? When can I see him?"

"Whenever you feel up to it." He hated this part of the job but it had to be done. He sat alongside her. "I assume you occupy separate bedrooms?"

"Yes. He sometimes gets home very late from work and he snores…" She twisted a handkerchief in her hands.

"So is it usual for Mr Prentice to be out very late at night?" She nodded.

"What did your husband do?" It was oh so easy for him to slip into the past tense. He found if he did, then the grieving widow would eventually follow suit and it helped her to accept the loss - at least he hoped it did.

She looked at him, puzzled.

"For a job, I mean. What was his occupation?"

"Oh, he was a partner at MacAllistair and Prentice in the High Street, a Chartered Accountant. He worked very hard…" The tears began to make tracks down her cheeks.

"Would he usually walk home?"

She nodded. "He doesn't drive," she smiled faintly. "He never learned, you see. Always too busy. I had to drive him everywhere, except when it was work - then he used a taxi or the train."

"I see." The inspector was viewing a map of Perry Green in his head. The park was a long from the most direct route from the High Street to The Willows. "He was found in the park." She looked up at him again, her eyes different, harder. "Did he usually come home that way?"

"I don't know," her voice much firmer now, with an edge to it. "How should I know the route he used? All I know is he walked everywhere."

"I see you have two children," he said, nodding to some framed photographs on the wall featuring a fair-haired, handsome young man and a pretty teenage girl. "Are they still at home?" He kept his voice level and gentle.

She followed his gaze, "No. Scott is at university in Oxford and Geraldine is on a trip to Paris, she's back next weekend." She sighed and in a small voice said, "How am I going to tell them?"

"Would you mind if my sergeant had a look around? It's just routine, to fill in some background." She look surprised, but nodded and Cotteril left the room. "Just routine" the inspector thought; that covers a multitude of sins.

"Is Mr Prentice away from home on business often?"

"Not very often. He sometimes has to go up town to see clients and stops over if he's working late."

"Where would he stay if he's … 'up town' did you say? Would that be London?"

"Sorry, yes London. Oh, I don't know. I think they use a hotel somewhere in the West End, near all the restaurants and theatres. Larry would know."

"Larry?"

"Lawrence MacAllistair, his partner. We've known Larry forever, he's almost part of the family." Her voice was level now, the shock had subsided and answering the questions gave her something to focus on, a purpose. "Would you mind if I get a cup of coffee?"

"I'll get it," the WPC said and headed to the kitchen.

"Is there anyone we can contact for you?"

She shook her head. "Larry will come over. Does he know yet?"

"No. We will talk to Mr MacAllistair later. Leave it to us, we'll make sure he knows as soon as possible." Greenwold took a deep breath. "As it is a suspicious death, I'm afraid a post-mortem will have to be carried out - you do understand?"

She nodded.

Sergeant Cotteril rejoined them and WPC Cane returned with two cups of coffee on a tray.

She stood. "I think I would like to see him now."

"If you're sure?" the inspector asked.

She nodded, "I'm sure."

"WPC Crane will take you in her car."

Chapter 3

After Mrs Prentice had identified her husband's body and been led away by the ever comforting WPC Crane, Colin was able to begin his post-mortem.

Never one to wait patiently at these times, Inspector Greenwold was back at the mortuary as soon as he had arranged for Mrs Prentice's statement to be taken.

"Any initial thoughts, Colin?"

"Plenty. He was stabbed once, very forcibly, in the chest." He pointed to the wound. "The knife has a six-inch blade and went in right up to the hilt. There are no signs of a struggle, no defensive wounds." He pointed to Mr Prentice's cut-free arms. "He was killed almost immediately by one solid blow. The time of death I would put at between twelve midnight and twelve-thirty this morning.

"The knife," he held up a bag with the weapon in, "is of a type that can be bought almost anywhere. It's just a kitchen knife. I suspect it is very, very common.

"His clothes are being thoroughly examined but I don't hold out a lot of hope of finding anything to connect to the murderer. SOCO are still searching the crime scene for evidence, but again I do not hold out a lot of hope.

"There are lots of small items being recovered but so far they have proved to be of no use, just litter." He took a breath and leant against the table occupied by the late Mr Prentice and continued: "He was on a tarmac path and the weather had been warm, so there isn't much chance of finding any footprints.

"If I had to hazard a guess, I would say that his assailant walked up to him, thrust the knife in and walked away again.

"You'll have my report once I have the results from the scene and his clothes. I very much doubt I'll have anything to add." He crossed his arms.

The inspector sighed heavily. "So, a perfect crime then?

"There's no such thing. Whoever it is will have given himself away somehow."

When Greenwold returned from the mortuary, he addressed those present in the squad room. "Ok people, all we have so far is that Mr Brian Prentice was stabbed to death at around midnight last night and his assailant appears to have got away without leaving a shred of evidence. He still had a large amount of money and, as far as we know, all his credit cards. So this was either personal or, worse, entirely random.

"We need to know everything about his background. He was a partner at MacAllistair and Prentice in the High Street. He has a wife, Helen Prentice, and two children, Scott and Geraldine who are out of town at the moment." He looked around, "or are they? Let's confirm that shall we?

"Sergeant Cotteril and I will interview his business partner. I want you to find out as much as you can about him and the rest of the family.

"Also, someone may have seen the attacker entering or leaving the park last night. I want some of you out there asking around and knocking on local resident's doors. Arrange that will you, McGuire?" The portly shape of DS McGuire rose from the edge of the desk he had been occupying and nodded.

"Let's get this cleared up quickly. The more we do before the news breaks, the better. Come on then, what are you waiting here for?" he clapped his hands at them, chivvying them up.

Turning to Cotteril he asked: "Do we know who found the body?"

"It was a Mr Groome of number 5, Tennyson Avenue. He was out walking his dog."

"Has Mr Groome given a statement?"

"Yes, sir, McGuire took it, I'll go and get it."

"Never mind," he said, stopping Cotteril as he turned to go. "I would like to talk to Mr Groome myself.

"Tennyson Avenue you say? That's not far from MacAllistair and Prentice is it?

"We'll see him first, then go on to see Mr MacAllistair."

Tennyson Avenue was lined with Victorian semi-detached houses with short front lawns. Halfway along it was the Kings Arms where Sergeant Cotteril drank on many an occasion. Mr Groome's house was at the far end of the road behind a neatly kept hedge and equally neat lawn. Cotteril rang the bell and the door opened almost immediately.

"Mr Groome?" he asked, holding out his warrant card. "I am DS Cotteril and this is DI Greenwold. May we come in?"

"I knew you were here," the old man said, holding the door open for them to enter. "Jackie heard you coming. To the left there," he said, indicating an open door. As they entered the living room, he shuffled, partly stooped, behind them.

"Jackie?" the inspector asked.

"My dog Jackie. Here boy," he called. A white and tan Jack Russell Terrier rushed into the room and up to Sergeant Cotteril who bent to stroke him. "Would you like a cuppa? The kettle's on." He went out to the kitchen and they heard him readying the cups. "Sit yourselves down," he called through. "Shan't be a tick."

The room was quite light and airy, not at all what you would expect from meeting the owner. The three-piece suite was new and of a modern design. The dining table in the window alcove was of a light coloured wood with two chairs at it. A fireplace dominated the wall adjoining his neighbour's, the mantelpiece groaning under the weight of the framed photographs that lined it. A television sat in the corner with just one armchair arranged to view it, its twin was turned away from it. A matching settee stood against the opposite wall that Sergeant Cotteril sat on and Jackie immediately jumped up into his lap.

"You've found a new friend there," Mr Groome said as he walked in with a tray in his hands. Inspector Greenwold took it from him and set it on the table. "I brought some biscuits. You coppers always like a nice cup of tea and a biscuit or two, am I right?" he smiled.

He was in his late sixties, Greenwold estimated; dressed in a shirt and tie, covered by a sleeveless pullover, grey trousers and tartan slippers. "Thank you very much," he said as he took the offered cup and a biscuit and sat down.

"I suppose you want me to tell you how I found him this morning," he said, plonking down in the other chair. "Well, Jackie and I were on our usual early morning walk. I always take him down the High Street, calling in at Mr Patel's for my paper, and then on into the park where I let him have a run around." He took a slurp of the hot tea then continued. "If it's nice, like today, I like to sit a while and watch Jackie running all over and just, what's the expression they use these days? Chill?"

"Chill out," Cotteril supplied.

"Yeah, that's it. Chill out. Well I didn't get much time to chill out today. No sooner had my bum hit the seat than Jackie started up barking. I went to see what the noise was all about and found the dead man in the middle of the path."

"Did you see anyone else in the park or maybe in the High Street?"

He shook his head, "No. Didn't see anyone except Mr Patel in his shop. Never do until Old Tom the milkman does his rounds. That's later."

"Did you touch the man, to see if he was dead or anything?"

"No. Touch nothing, that's what I thought. Don't touch nothing - just call the police. So I got Jackie and went back to Patel's and used his phone."

"Did you see anyone while you were on your way to make the call?"

He shook his head again. "No. Sorry."

Inspector Greenwold drained his cup and stood. "Well thank you, Mr Groome, we appreciate your time and the tea and biscuit."

At the door Inspector Greenwold turned to him. "You live alone?"

"Yeah, since my Dawnie passed on ten years ago. There's just me an' Jackie now, ain't that right boy?" The dog barked on cue and wagged its stump of a tail.

"Well, thank you again," Greenwold said as they stepped outside.

Chapter 4

The offices of MacAllistair and Prentice occupied the second floor of a sparkling new building on the corner of the High Street and River Gardens. It was all glass and stainless steel with an atrium that was so shiny it hurt the eyes.

A smartly dressed woman in her early twenties sat behind a curved reception desk. She looked up as the men entered and smiled brightly at them.

"Good morning sirs, can I help you?"

"Yes, we would like to talk to Mr MacAllistair please."

"Do you have an appointment?" she said, the smile not moving - her teeth were impossibly white.

"I'm afraid not. We are here on official business." He held out his warrant card for her. With the smile still in place, she typed a number into the phone pad next to her and spoke into a headset that they had totally failed to see.

"Mr MacAllistair? I'm sorry to disturb you sir, but I have two gentlemen from Perry Green police here to see you." She listened, her eyes moving as if she were reading what was being said. "He will be down to see you directly. Would you please take a seat," she indicated the black leather armchairs and sofas arranged along one wall. "Can I get you something to drink? A tea or a coffee?"

"No thank you," Inspector Greenwold replied as they sat on what appeared to be a new sofa. "Have you been in these offices long?"

She looked up from her computer screen. "Oh no. Just six months. We used to have offices above two shops further down the High Street."

"How long have you worked for MacAllistair and Prentice?"

"A couple of years."

"Do you know Mr MacAllistair or Mr Prentice at all?"

"Not really, they often talk to me when they're not hurrying by; they're very nice like that. But I don't really know them."

A lift door opened and a very smart, very tall man strode into the reception area, a welcoming smile on his face. "Gentlemen, I am Lawrence MacAllistair. How can I help you?" He held out his hand and the inspector and sergeant shook it in turn.

"May we talk somewhere in private please, sir. It is on a very important matter."

"Certainly." He turned to the receptionist. "Sandra, is the boardroom free?"

"Yes, Mr MacAllistair."

"Thank you. Has Mr Prentice arrived in this morning?"

"Not yet, sir."

"Well, when he comes in would you tell him where we are and ask him to join us please?"

"Yes sir."

"This way gentlemen." MacAllistair led them to a set of highly polished double doors set into one wall of the reception area.

Inside, a huge teak table sat in the middle of the room and arranged around it were padded matching chairs. MacAllistair pulled a chair out half way down the far side of the table and sat down, waving the two men to chairs opposite.

"Now, gentlemen, what can I do for you?"

"When was the last time you saw Mr Prentice?"

He frowned, "Last night. Before I went home. Is this about Brian? What happened?"

"At what time was that, sir?"

"At about seven o'clock…" He paused, "yes, a quarter to seven. I remember looking at the clock in reception as I left the building. Brian was coming out of the boardroom, this room. He had been holding a meeting with some clients."

"Would these be new clients that he was with?"

"No. We have been representing Carters for many years. It was just a regular portfolio meeting." He leant forward. "Has something happened to Brian?"

"I'm sorry to have to tell you, Mr MacAllistair, that Mr Prentice was found in the park this morning. He had been murdered."

MacAllistair's face drained of blood, his mouth opened and shut several times but no sound came out. Finally he shook himself and regained the use of his voice. "Our Mr Prentice? Are you sure?"

"He has been formally identified by his wife. It happened around midnight on the path through the park. He had been walking, alone we think, when his attacker struck."

"He's dead?" The inspector nodded. "My Lord!" He sat back in the chair and took a small silver box from his waistcoat pocket. He opened it, took out a pill and popped it into his mouth. Reaching across the table to a bottle of mineral water, he poured some into a glass and swallowed it down. "Heart," he said by way of explanation. He composed himself.

"What about Helen, um Mrs Prentice? Does she know?"

"Yes, she identified him."

"How is she? Sorry, stupid question. Does she have someone with her?"

"One of our WPCs is with her for the moment."

"I must go to her, see if there's anything I can do. How awful! Poor Helen. Poor Brian," he added.

"If I might ask you some questions before you do, sir?"

"Yes. Of course. Anything, ask anything."

"Do you know what time Mr Prentice left the office last night?"

"No, but we sign in and out so it will be in the book on reception. Fire regulations you see, so that we know who is in the building if a fire starts." Cotteril stood and went out to retrieve it.

"Did you know if he was meeting someone after work last night? A client perhaps, or maybe someone from...?" he consulted his notes, "Carters'?"

"It is possible I suppose, but he never said anything to me."

"How well do you know Mr Prentice?"

He sighed, "Brian and I go back a long way. We both worked for an institution in town, Brian started there from university. We worked together on a few accounts and forged a friendship even though I am, as I expect you can see, a generation older than he.

"We decided to start out on our own and spent the first five years building this business up, working very closely together. I was best man at his wedding to Helen and am godfather to their children." He paused. "Oh my God, do Scott and Geraldine know?"

"They are not in town at the present."

"No, of course not. Gerri's in France isn't she. And I expect Scott's up at university, up to no good." He caught the inspector's expression. "Oh, I'm sorry. That was very indiscreet of me. You see, Scott has been a bit of a handful lately, causing poor Helen and Brian no end of stress. To be honest, when Sandra called me I thought you were here to see Brian about him. How awful."

Sergeant Cotteril reappeared with the book. "He signed out at eight-fifteen. Apparently there's night security here, I have the name and telephone number of the man on duty last night so that we can verify it."

"Thank you." He turned his attention back to MacAllistair who was staring at the table. "Sir, would you know if he would have met up with anyone else after work? An acquaintance maybe or…?" he left the question out there, hanging. MacAllistair collected his thoughts; he studied the desk a few seconds more and, with a slight cough of embarrassment spoke with a quieter, more confidential tone to the officers.

"Well, Inspector, I hope I can rely on your discretion but I have suspected for some time that things are not, how can I put it, all roses in the Prentice household."

"Sir?" Greenwold prompted.

"I *think*, and I must emphasise I have no proof of this but, I think Brian has been seeing someone else." He relaxed a little, as if a weight had been removed from him.

"Have you any idea who this might be, sir?"

He shook his head. "I'm sorry, no."

"How long have you suspected this?"

"About six months, but it may well have been going on for some time before that. He was very careful, I'm sure he wouldn't want to hurt anyone by his actions but… Well, he spent a lot of time at the office and became keen on going for a drink after work, regardless of the time. I assumed things were rough at home and he wanted to put off going there as long as possible. Then, I think six, or maybe more, months ago, he seemed to suddenly turn a corner.

"At first I thought he and Helen had patched things up and they were happy again, but then I noticed when he left work he headed off in a different direction than that of his home."

"Which direction would that be, sir?"

"Well, strangely enough, toward the park."

"And you have no idea of who this person is, sir?"

"Sorry. No. I wish I had."

Inspector Greenwold changed tack, "Do you know if Mr Prentice had any financial problems?"

MacAllistair looked genuinely surprised. "Why no, Inspector. He has a very good income from here and has some investments of his own. Oh, I know Gerri and Scott are a drain on his resources - just as all teenagers are - but I'm sure his finances were sound."

"Does Mrs Prentice work at all, do you know?"

"No. Helen gave up her career when Scott was born. She was a PA for a director at Grundy's the hotelier, but she never went back. Didn't need to, Brian and I were doing very well at the time. We had established a very good client list and were signing new clients regularly."

"How did he get on with everyone? Is there anyone you can think of who would like to do him harm?"

"Everybody loved him. He got on with absolutely everyone, that's why we have done so well, he is very good with people. I can't think of a single person who might want to say anything bad about him, let alone kill him."

"Do you know of any clubs or social haunts that Mr Prentice might have had?"

"He belonged to Whiteley's, the gentlemen's club in Parade Street. He liked to frequent a live music venue, oh what was it called now?"

"The Cellar Club?" Sergeant Cotteril supplied.

"That's it! The Cellar Club. But I don't think he's been there in oh, a year or so now. No, Whiteley's is the only one I can think of. Maybe June would know if there were more." He looked at their blank expressions. "Sorry, June is … was Brian's secretary. No doubt you will want to talk to her as well?"

"Thank you, yes we would."

June turned out to be a very pleasant fifty-year-old woman, very efficient and forthcoming. But she had nothing to add to that already supplied by MacAllistair. She took the news badly and had to be taken home by a colleague. Inspector Greenwold and Sergeant Cotteril thanked MacAllistair for his time and took their leave of him.

Their journey back to the station took them along the High Street, the oldest part of town. Once it had been just a church, a coaching house and collection of cottages along a major route into the sprawl of London. When the canal was built to the West, many of the navigators who toiled on its construction settled there.

The major growth came in the 1950s when, like many small towns and villages, it was designated a "satellite town" and built up to take the strain off the capital city.

Businesses moved with their workers into the countryside for a better way of life than the inner city could provide and Perry Green grew. Not quite a "Garden City", but it still retained a good deal of its open spaces that were put to good use by making them into playing fields for football, cricket and rugby.

The park where Mr Prentice had been discovered had only tennis courts to interrupt its greenery. As they drove up to it, they both glanced at the entrance to where the tape was still very much in evidence.

"Pull over, I want to have a look at the scene of the crime again."

Cotteril did as he was bid and they climbed out of the car and started walking along the path.

It was getting toward dusk but the street lamps dotted along the path had not switched on yet. A lone constable raised the tape for them to pass under it.

"When did the circus leave town?" Greenwold asked him.

"Sir?"

"SOCO. When did they pack up and go?"

He looked at his watch. "About three hours ago now, sir. There hasn't been anybody here since."

They walked on, retracing Prentice's steps.

"Even at midnight he would have ample time to see someone coming toward him." He turned again to the constable who was stamping some life into his aching feet.

"Are all the lamps working?"

"Yes sir, except the very last one at the far end, that one blew about a week ago. I walk across here every night," he added to qualify his answer.

Greenwold continued his slow walk. It was a hundred yards to where a tributary path headed at right angles toward the tennis courts. There was no cover between where the officers walked and there, the bushes and trees starting at the far side of the junction. He stopped and looked around.

"The ground was hard, we've had no rain for quite a while," he said to himself. "It was a cloudless night as I remember, a bit chilly.

"He must have seen his attacker approach him but made no effort to run."

"How do you know that, sir?"

"The way he was facing. He was facing home. Either the attacker drew no attention to himself or Prentice knew him."

"Could it have been more than one?" Cotteril asked.

Greenwold nodded, pursing his lips. "Possibly. But this wasn't a mugging gone wrong, we know that."

"He could have fought them off and they knifed him in the heat of the moment?" Cotteril suggested.

"Colin said there was no sign of a struggle. No defensive wounds. No, whoever it was just walked up to him and thrust the knife in."

They stood in silence for a while then Greenwold shivered. "Come on, you could do with an early night and I have some sleep to catch up on. You get off home; I'll walk back to the station from here. See you in the morning, Sergeant."

"Goodnight, sir."

That evening Inspector Greenwold flopped down into his favourite reclining chair and sighed deeply. He operated the handle that raised his feet on a padded section so that he was almost horizontal. He reached out and picked up the crystal glass with his favourite whiskey, it had been a long day.

Questions. That was it. Questions. As he contemplated his left big toe poking cheekily through the hole in his sock, he pondered the nature of his profession. You ask questions, you get answers; they may be good, they may be bad, they may be true or false, but you got answers. Answers lead to more questions, which, in turn lead to more answers, and so it goes until... Until there are no more questions to ask, then you have it. You know everything there is to know. Then all you have to do is sort it all out. Filter out the irrelevant, focus on the relevant. With all the data, there can be only one solution.

Ten minutes later he was snoring gently. The whiskey glass had fallen from his hand, spilling its contents on the rug around his chair, specifically put there by Mrs Greenwold for that very purpose. This had happened so often that the rug was now 40% proof and to go near it with a naked flame was taking your life into your hands.

Chapter 5

At just after eleven o'clock the next day McGuire ambled into the incident room. Greenwold looked up enquiringly from the statements in his hand.

"Yes?" he asked as McGuire divested himself of his too small jacket. He wouldn't admit that he had gained weight, let alone buy larger clothes. He hitched his trousers up, his paunch having rolled them down to his hips.

"He has three accounts active, all at different banks," he said without preamble. Opening his notebook he flipped through the pages. "The first is his usual cheque account that his pay goes into and that all the household bills are paid from.

"The second is fed from the first with what's left over, that's like his disposable income account if you like. All very straight forward so far." He flipped a page over.

"The last account has had several very large payments made into it at irregular intervals from an account in Ireland. From this one, a regular payment is going out to a property management company."

"Do we know the name of this company?"

"Woodwell's in the High Street. I've been in touch with them and the payments are rent on a maisonette in Drover Way." He let the locale sink in then added, "It overlooks the park."

Greenwold nodded. "Do you know where these payments into this account are coming from?"

"Ah, no, not yet. But I will soon," he added.

"Do you have the address for this maisonette?"

"Twenty-eight, Drover Way. Very nice. I reckon he's got a bit on the side stashed there."

"Quite possibly. While we find out, I want you to carry on digging. I want to know where he's getting the money. Rents aren't cheap there."

McGuire looked deflated, he wouldn't have minded a visit to Drovers Way himself. "Ok chief."

The "apartments", as the management company called them, in Drover Way were very recent builds to a high specification and aimed at young business folk who commuted into London each day. They were in a gated road and number 28 looked very much like number 27 and not dissimilar to number 29. In fact, they were identical boxes stacked one upon another. Very neat and shiny boxes it has to be said, but soulless.

When the door was opened in answer to Sergeant Cotteril's press on the bell, he stepped backwards. The young woman standing before him was beautiful: blond hair tied back in a pony tail, bright blue eyes, her slim figure was clad in skin-tight jeans and a loose sweatshirt with the sleeves rolled up.

"Yes?" she asked, a smile playing on her lips, suggesting that she was well aware of the effect she was having on Cotteril's libido.

Inspector Greenwold stepped into the breach. "DI Greenwold and DS Cotteril of Perry Green CID," he said, holding out his warrant card. "May we come in?"

"Have I done anything wrong?" she asked.

"Not to my knowledge."

"Then please do come in." She stood aside to let the inspector and the gaping sergeant pass.

"Do close your mouth, Sergeant." Greenwold said and was rewarded by a light laugh from the girl.

"Who is it?" enquired a voice from upstairs.

"It's the Police," she answered. "They've come to arrest me."

"What?" A young man came down; it was obvious they were brother and sister from their hair colouring and delicate features. "I'm sorry," he said, "you are?"

"DI Greenwold and DS Cotteril of Perry Green CID and might I ask your names?"

"Katie and Stephen Watkins. What can we do for you, Inspector?"

"May we go through?" Greenwold asked, nodding to the open door to the lounge.

"Pardon my brother's manners, Inspector. Do go through, would you like some tea? I've seen it on TV that all policemen like a cup of tea at the home of the… What am I? The victim? The culprit?"

"Be your age, Katie. Sorry about her, Inspector, she's a sucker for a uniform."

"I'm not wearing a uniform, sir."

Oh yes you are, Cotteril thought. It screams "copper" at anyone who sees it.

They went through to the lounge and sat down. It was sparingly decorated and furnished too young for Greenwold's taste. There were a series of photographs that caught the eye as they were in a place of prominence. Greenwold could only make out the nearest, it appeared to be a group photograph of some skiers. Stephen, who was playing the host, interrupted.

"Tea? Coffee? We have both, straight and decaf. What would you like?" he smiled benevolently.

"I'll have a tea, as it comes, with two sugars," Inspector Greenwold replied.

"Coffee please, milk no sugar," Cotteril answered. "Thank you."

"This *is* exciting," Katie enthused. "I've never had a real policeman in my home before. Are you on a "case" at the moment? Are we suspects?" Her eyes sparkled with excitement.

"Do you know a Mr Brian Prentice?" There was the clatter of a teaspoon being dropped in the kitchen.

"Yes?" she said guardedly.

"Could you tell me how you know him?"

Stephen had come back into the lounge. "He's a friend. We met a few years ago on a skiing holiday in France, why?"

"I'm sorry to have to tell you that he was found yesterday morning in the park. He had been murdered."

The colour drained from Katie's face, Stephen sat by her side and hugged her.

"I'm sorry to have to be the bearer of such bad news, but I thought it better that you heard it from us rather than the newspapers."

"But, how did you know to come and tell us?" Stephen asked.

"During the course of our investigations we discovered that Mr Prentice was paying the rent on this flat." He turned to Katie.

"When was the last time you saw Mr Prentice?"

She looked at Stephen who shrugged. "The night before last. He was here … visiting."

"And where were you, sir?"

"I was here as well."

The inspector paused, but only momentarily. "At what time did Mr Prentice leave?"

They looked at one another. "About midnight I suppose," Katie said. Stephen nodded in agreement.

"Could you be more precise, miss?

Again, the conferring glance, then Stephen said, "Ten-to. I remember the program we were watching hadn't quite ended when he said he would have to go.

"After we had said goodnight and come back in, the adverts were on. The next program was due to start at midnight."

Katie asked: "You said he was found yesterday morning, what time?"

"Five-thirty, a man walking his dog found him."

"Where?" Stephen asked.

"On the footpath. About fifty yards from the High Street entrance. The coroner puts the time of death at between midnight and twelve-thirty."

"Oh my God! He had just left us!" She buried her face in Stephen's shoulder.

Sergeant Cotteril's phone rang and he stepped out into the hallway to answer it.

"I'm sorry, miss, but I am going to have to ask you to come down to the station to make a statement. You too, sir, if you don't mind."

"No, not at all. Now?"

He looked at his watch; it was one-thirty. "Shall we say later this afternoon? When you feel up to it."

"Sir?" Sergeant Cotteril had reappeared at the door and had an urgent expression on his face.

"Just coming. Thank you for the drinks and we're sorry to have to leave you with such sad news. We'll see ourselves out. Good day."

When they stepped outside Cotteril said, "That was McGuire, he's found out where Prentice got the money."

McGuire had a smug expression on his face and was feigning being casual.

"It appears Mr Prentice had some kind of dodge going on.

"The account feeding his third account here is in the name of MacAllistair and Prentice in Dublin," he continued.

Greenwold sat in a chair facing him. "Go on," he prompted.

"I'm not sure, but it seems that every now and then, not with any kind of regularity, a payment made by one of their clients goes to this account instead of the real MacAllistair and Prentice account in London. Never a very large sum, but big enough."

"So, basically, he is using it to fund a love-nest he has set up in Drover Way. Is that it?"

"Looks that way."

"I wonder if MacAllistair knew what he was doing?" Greenwold pondered.

"I wouldn't have thought so, chief. Wouldn't make sense."

Cotteril piped up: "Perhaps MacAllistair found out. Maybe he confronted Prentice and…"

"Nah, that don't wash," McGuire countered. "Why kill him when all he had to do was turn him in? My money's on the wife; she finds out about his extra-curricular activities and, in a fit of rage, kills him."

"Hmm, that doesn't quite gel with the crime scene though, does it?" Cotteril parried. "That wasn't a rage killing. It was cold and calculated.

"Wouldn't she confront him first, have a row. Then snatch up whatever is to hand and…" Cotteril made stabbing motions reminiscent of the shower scene in *Psycho*.

"Why not just divorce him? Take him to the cleaners. Anyway, I thought you said she was wiped out by his death?"

Cotteril thought a moment. "What about the lover? Perhaps he had called it off and had given her her marching orders?"

"Then why did it happen in the park?" McGuire asked. "You'd expect that it would happen at the flat or somewhere not so close to her doorstep if she'd planned it."

They went silent and the inspector decided it was time to get them back on track.

"This is all good conjecture, but we haven't explored all the possibilities yet," he said. "What about the son and daughter? The boy sounds like he could get himself in trouble and maybe the old man wasn't coming through with the money any more."

He stood and clapped his hands, the others in the room stopped what they were doing. "Listen up everybody, we have some work to do. I want to know all about Scott and Geraldine Prentice.

"Where they are, what they do, and if they are in money - or other - difficulties."

"I also want to know if MacAllistair has something to hide. Does he have a similar account in Ireland? Maybe they were both in on it?"

"How about Mrs Prentice, what does she do all day? She hasn't a job, the kids are off her hands, the old man is at work or play all day and most of the night. What does she get up to?

"I also want to know if anyone saw anything on the night in question. How did the door-to-door go?"

"Drew a blank, sir," PC Moore said. "The park's too far away from the houses to get any casual sightings and no one was walking their dog at midnight."

"But were there any drunks on their way home? Any star-crossed lovers getting down and dirty in the shelter? Any druggies looking to score that may have stumbled over the event? Let's get back out there, use a bit of..."

"Lateral thinking, sir?"

"Thank you, Sergeant, lateral thinking. Get out there and get information. Go!"

Chapter 6

The next morning, Greenwold was shaken awake by his wife. "Joe? The phone. The phone's ringing." He stirred himself and picked up the handset.

"Yes?"

"Sir," came Cotteril's urgent voice at the other end of the line. "There's been another one."

Greenwold was wide-awake. "When?"

"Late last night we think. Colin's down there now."

"Where is it?" He scribbled the address on a pad on the night-stand. "I'll be there in twenty minutes." He hung up the phone.

The crime scene was in a block of garages that serviced neighbouring high-rise flats. By the time the inspector arrived there were people at every available space on the balconies. The area had been cordoned off and two men were remonstrating heatedly with the constable who wouldn't let them collect their cars to get to work.

Colin was walking away from the covered form on the concrete. "I had to call you, Joe, it's the same MO."

"What?"

"A single blow as far as I can make out. The murder weapon was left in the body."

"Who discovered it?"

"That man over there with the green fleece jacket."

Greenwold strode over to the man, "I understand you discovered the deceased?"

"Yeah. I came down to go to work and he was lying just in front of Jack's garage."

"Did you see anyone else around?"

"No, nobody. I start early, see. I'm a milkman."

"What did you do, did you touch him?"

"Well yes, I turned him over."

"Why?"

"We get some winos round here. I thought it was just one of them, passed out like. Then I saw the knife sticking out of him an' I recognised him."

"You know who the victim is?"

"Yeah. It's Dave from number 132. His garage is a few doors down from Jack's."

"And Jack is?"

"He's my neighbour." He turned and pointed to a squat man wearing a blue quilted anorak. "That's him, Jack Whitman."

"And you are?"

"Tony French, I live at number 118, the floor below Dave. I don't know his surname, but Jack might."

"Did you touch anything else on the dead man? Think hard."

"No. When I saw the knife that was it for me. I ran an' called you lot."

"Thank you, you will need to make a full statement. Would you go with the sergeant here and he will take it."

As Cotteril escorted the man back to his car, Greenwold made his way over to Jack Whitman. "I understand you knew the deceased?"

"Yeah, that's right." He was short, only five foot six by Greenwold's estimate, and had the appearance of a frightened rabbit caught in the headlights of an oncoming juggernaut.

"Do you know the deceased's name?"

"Yes, it's Dave. Dave Quinn, number 132."

"Do you know if Mr Quinn had any friends or visitors round last night?"

"Wouldn't know. I've only met him washing the car or on the stairs, just to nod to, like.

"But you know his name?"

"Oh yeah, we introduced ourselves first time."

"Thank you, Mr Whitman. We will also need a statement from you, if you wouldn't mind going over to that car the sergeant there will take it."

Greenwold walked back to where Colin was standing, supervising the removal of the body.

"Is it the same style of knife?"

"No a different one, but it still looks a very common brand of kitchen knife."

"Are you sure it's the same killer?"

"I can't be until I get him back to the mortuary, but I would think it highly likely."

"Time of death?"

"Around ten-thirty last night, plus or minus an hour. I'll give you a more accurate time later."

"Who's the senior officer here after us?"

"Sergeant Howes over there." He indicated a uniformed officer.

"Thanks, see you back at the factory."

Greenwold took Sergeant Howes aside. "Colin says time of death was around ten-thirty last night. There's a good chance someone saw or heard something. We need a door-to-door started."

"All ready started, sir. I have ten men, one to each floor, going round the block now."

"And the houses at the bottom of the driveway?"

"Another five down there, but I doubt we'll get anything, even at that hour. People in flats don't tend to look out of their windows much, especially at night. And they generally have the telly on so loud we're out all night telling them to turn them down."

Greenwold looked up at all the faces peering down on the scene. The flats were relatively new and still well looked after, the people living here had not lost their pride in their neighbourhood.

The garages were tidy and free from rubbish, there was evidence that the taps at the far end were working and used frequently from the large damp patch around them. His eyes roamed over the white suited men examining the ground.

He called Sergeant Howes over again. "Has anyone informed the next of kin?"

"Lived alone, sir, since his divorce. We're tracking down his ex-wife now."

"Let me know as soon as you find her I would like to interview her."

"Where will you be?"

"Contact me at the station."

In the squad room that afternoon Greenwold clapped his hands to bring the officers to order. "People, people. Ok, let's see how this fits with the Prentice murder.

"Has anyone got anything from the neighbours?"

"Yes sir, they say they thought he was a suicide waiting to happen," PC Moore said. "He couldn't get over the break-up of his marriage, he worshipped his wife."

There were a few sniggers from behind him.

"Let's keep this adult, shall we?" the inspector admonished them. "Anything else we know about him?"

"He liked his beer. Stopped off at the Kings Arms on the way home from work every night for just the one pint. Sat by himself at the bar, talked a lot to Sally, the barmaid there."

"If he just had the one, why was he in the garages at…" he looked at the report from Colin, "at ten-fifteen? Was he just

34

getting home? Or was he going out again? Can we trace his movements leading up to his death?"

"Yes, sir," DS Briant said. "He left the Kings at the usual time but stopped off at the Regal in Bowman Rise for a curry. A Chicken Tikka Masala to be precise. He ate alone and didn't look like he had been expecting anyone to join him. He paid up and left a good tip. Seems he's a regular there.

"His car was just outside the restaurant and they saw him drive off in the direction of his home at ten o'clock on the dot. They have a chiming clock just inside the door."

"Any luck with the door-to-door?"

"Only one person said they thought they heard a shout at about the time in question, sir. But they didn't investigate, better not to these days." A few murmurs of agreement came from the room.

"The knife," Greenwold pointed to a photograph on the board, "is a six-inch blade kitchen knife you can find in most supermarkets up and down the country. No prints as before. SOCO are still at the scene, but I don't hold out a lot of hope there. There was no sign of a struggle. He was killed with a single blow to the chest that buried the knife up to the hilt. Colin says he was probably dead before he hit the ground.

"The interesting thing is, it is quite hard to get knife to go that far in unless it is turned so that the blade is horizontal." He demonstrated with a ruler. "The person who carried out this, *and* the murder of Mr Prentice appears to know what he's doing."

"Have we got a serial killer on our patch, sir?" WPC Allen asked from the rear of the room.

"I sincerely hope not. We will need to release a statement to the papers soon, but we'll leave the press office to deal with that. We have not as yet determined any connection between the two.

"Prentice was a businessman. Quinn worked for a hi-tech company, Cyntex Systems. Prentice was forty-eight, married with two children, with a bit on the side. Quinn was thirty-three, divorced and suicidal. As far as we know, they never met.

"I want to know Quinn's background. From which school he attended to which way he voted in the election. Do we know his financial situation? No? Let's get onto that then. We know Prentice was skimming his company, was Quinn up to anything similar?

"Where is Quinn's estranged wife? We need to know her movements for the time of death. How did the divorce go? We know Quinn was devastated but was he holding out on her in some way? Anything I've missed? Good. Off you go then."

As the room cleared Cotteril passed Greenwold a cup of tea.

"Thank you," he said absently. "What's the connection, Sergeant? What's the connection?"

"They were both killed by the same man," he smiled weakly.

"Thank you for your considered opinion." He shuffled through some files in front of him. "Have we had the lovely Katie and her brother in for statements yet?"

"Yes sir, they came in yesterday. They're in the file." He handed Greenwold yet another file for his collection.

"Have we interviewed the Prentice offspring?"

"Not yet."

"No? We have taken our eye off the ball, Sergeant." He noticed Cotteril's guilty expression.

"Oh I'm berating myself as well as you. We've been thrown by the Quinn murder. Let's get it back on track. You find out about the son and daughter while I have another word with MacAllistair."

Chapter 7

Inspector Greenwold was shown into MacAllistair's office by the ever-efficient June. It appeared that both MacAllistair and Prentice shared her as a secretary; such was her knowledge and understanding of the business.

"Mr MacAllistair will be with you shortly, Inspector. Is there anything I can get you?"

"No thank you. But I wouldn't mind five minutes of your time."

"Oh!" She looked scared but sat down next to him.

"You knew Mr Prentice very well I understand."

"Yes, I had been with him, and Mr MacAllistair, for some years."

"Did he ever take you into his confidence over personal matters? You know, unburden himself to you?"

She immediately looked defensive and wary. "Well, sometimes, if I made a comment about him being preoccupied. But he would never just use me to "unburden" himself. He wasn't a selfish man. He thought more of others than he did of himself."

"But you would have been aware of the problems that his son was causing? His, shall we say, misguided ways?" Greenwold said, playing a hunch.

"Oh, you know about that?"

"We are very thorough in our inquiries."

"I see. Yes. Scott, Mr Prentice's son, was a great deal of trouble to Mr Prentice, along with his sister.

"I believe he, on more than one occasion, got in with the wrong sort of people and Mr Prentice had to sort it out.

"He came here on one occasion demanding money to "bail him out" he said. I couldn't help overhearing, Scott was never one to keep his voice down and he was very aggressive in his demands."

"Did you hear the amount being discussed on that occasion?"

"Oh yes. I remember being quite taken aback. I mean, you expect children to come to you for the odd ten or twenty pounds, and when in dire consequences maybe fifty or a hundred. But Scott was asking, no demanding, a thousand pounds.

"Oh, Mr Prentice shushed him but both myself and, I believe, Mr MacAllistair heard him. A thousand pounds," she repeated incredulously.

"You mentioned Scott's sister, Geraldine, being part of the burden Mr Prentice carried? She seemed to be the sort of daughter most parents dream about having." He was baiting her and not very subtly, but she went for it.

"Oh she was just as bad, but in a very different way.

"With her it was all "keeping up appearances". She *had* to have the latest designer clothes. She *had* to go abroad with her friends twice a year. She *had* to go to the best private schools." It was obvious June was onto her favourite peeve so it was with reluctance that Inspector Greenwold had to suspend the conversation when MacAllistair entered the room. She immediately looked flushed and made her excuses and left very quickly. MacAllistair looked bemused.

"What *have* you been doing to poor June, Inspector?"

"Sir?"

"She looked quite distraught."

"We were discussing the shortcomings of the National Health Service, sir."

"Oh yes, she does rather get emotional about that. Her mother is in a nursing home you see, and the expense, well, we've had to help June. Not in a monetary way you understand, but in advice and speaking to the right people on her behalf.

"Now, Inspector, how can I help you further?"

"How is Mrs Prentice, sir?"

"Oh, she's understandably very upset. We all are, but I just can't imagine what she is going through."

"Do the children know yet? Scott and Geraldine?"

"Oh yes. They're home with her now."

"In the course of our investigations we have been delving into Mr Prentice's finances."

"Oh? Why would you do that?"

"Just routine, sir. He may have been being blackmailed and the murder a result of a payoff going wrong. Just one avenue of investigation we are pursuing."

"Of course. I wouldn't have thought of that. Yes, I see." MacAllistair lapsed into a thoughtful silence. Greenwold didn't break it, there was more coming, he could feel it.

"Is that really a possibility, Inspector? The blackmail I mean?"

"It is one theory that meets the facts, sir. The killer was very clever, he didn't leave a trace." Again the thoughtful silence. Come on you bugger, the inspector urged to himself. Come *on*.

"Inspector." He leant forward conspiratorially. "I am determined to help you in any way I can to bring Brian's killer to justice. That being so, I can save you some time in your investigations where Brian's finances are concerned."

Greenwold breathed a sigh of relief to himself.

"His children, Scott and that awful Geraldine, were bleeding him dry.

"On more than one occasion he came to me for advice, but really to borrow from the company." He sat back and spread his hands; the body language said, "I am being painfully open with you."

"Naturally we documented it and he paid interest on the loan, although I must say it was punitive interest." He stood and, clasping his hands behind his back, walked to the window. He stood for a few moments then looked down and sighed. Turning, he said, "Inspector, I know that Brian was taking money from the business." The relief of finally admitting it to someone was clearly visible on his face. "It wasn't really a very clever way of doing it, but it was effective. I would say he had had seventy thousand out of the company to date."

"And you did nothing about it?" He had committed a crime, Greenwold thought, and you didn't tell us.

"No, Inspector." He sat again, agitated. "As I have told you, Brian and I go back a long way. I felt I could help him if he came to me but if I let on I knew what was happening, he would certainly resign and may even turn himself over to the authorities." And we can't have that, can we, Greenwold thought ruefully.

"He had to see sense for himself. Someone confronting him wouldn't do it."

"So you knew he was embezzling money from the company accounts?"

MacAllistair sagged. "Yes, Inspector, I did."

Greenwold leant forward now, a mean look on his face. "I could arrest you now, sir, for aiding and abetting. The Inland Revenue would not look very kindly on your actions. What you have admitted to me could destroy all that you have worked to build up.

"Now I have to ask myself, do I really believe you wouldn't realise this? Do I really think you are that naive?" He let the questions hang in the air between them.

After a silence in which he could hear his hair growing, the inspector was about to prompt MacAllistair when he caved in.

"I did have an ulterior motive, but to reveal it would…"

"Make you a suspect?"

MacAllistair winced as he said it. "Yes," he admitted. He sat back, not meeting the inspector's eye.

"I am in love with Helen. There, I've said it." Probably for the first time, Greenwold thought. "I have been infatuated with her since, oh forever. But I could never hurt Brian let alone kill him. You have to believe that, Inspector," he pleaded.

Questions, the inspector thought. There are more questions now. Like, what about your wife, Mr MacAllistair? How did you think you were going to win Helen from her husband? Did you have a plan in mind? Did it include murder? Or, more like it, ruination? Yes, that's more like it. That's the pen-pushers way. Use money to destroy your enemy. Wars were won nowadays by bringing countries to their knees with sanctions instead of meeting on the battlefield.

"Do you know a Mr David Quinn?"

"What? Who?" MacAllistair was totally thrown by the change in direction. "I … I don't think so. No, I'm sure I've never heard the name, why? What has he to do with Brian's death?"

"Just another line of inquiry." Inspector Greenwold stood to leave. "I would appreciate it if you would present yourself at the station to make a statement. Today."

"Will you be pressing charges?"

"That, as I'm sure you know, sir, would be in the hands of the Crown Prosecution Service, but as you are a wholly owned company and the only "victim" of your complicity is your own company I wouldn't expect so." MacAllistair breathed a sigh of relief. "But, that is not for me to say," Greenwold continued. "The CPS may view it differently. So if you wouldn't mind, sir. Today, at the station. Good day."

Chapter 8

Before arriving at 23, The Willows, Cotteril had spent some very fruitful time on the phone with an opposite number in the Oxford constabulary. It seemed young Master Scott Prentice was quite well known to them. But not as well known as he was to members of Oxford's drugs circle.

He tugged on the bell pull and within seconds heard someone pounding down the stairs. A young fresh-faced man who could only be Scott Prentice flung the door open: the familial resemblance was remarkable.

"Oh!" Scott seemed crestfallen. "Yes?"

Cotteril held up his warrant card. "DS Cotteril, Perry Green CID." Scott wasn't paying attention to the card; he was looking over Cotteril's shoulder as if he had been expecting someone else.

"Sorry?" he said, returning his gaze to the sergeant and then his card. "Oh!" a look of panic came into his eyes. "Err, yes. Come in, please, come in." He almost tugged Cotteril through the door. I think I would like to meet whoever you are expecting, Cotteril thought. This could be interesting.

"Scott Prentice?"

"Yes?"

"I would like to ask you some questions in connection with your father's death if you don't mind, sir?"

"Err, no. Fine. Yes. Come into the lounge, erm, would you like a cup of tea or something? I can…"

"No sir, I'm fine for now." They sat opposite one another.

Cotteril, by means of moving quicker than Scott expected, had stationed himself facing the front window where he could see anyone coming up the driveway. "Is your sister at home, sir? I would like to talk to her too."

"Oh, yes, Gerri's upstairs somewhere. Probably doing her hair. That's all she seems to do." He laughed nervously. He was a strikingly handsome young man but had the look of someone who could be a bit wild and irresponsible if the mood took him. For now, he was in "charm" mode.

"I would just like to offer my condolences to you, sir, and reassure you we will do everything in our power to bring your father's killer to justice."

That seemed to throw him, it was as if he didn't know what Cotteril was talking about, then realisation dawned and his whole attitude changed. "Thank you, Sergeant. It was a great shock to us all. We are all still trying to come to terms with it..." he finished, his voice cracking a little. Very good, Cotteril thought. Bravo. You should get an Oscar mate.

"I understand you were at university when it happened?"

"Yes. I was just hanging out with some friends there."

"Could I ask you your movements on the night in question. The night your father died?"

"Err, yes, sure. Um, oh yes. We had been to the Turf Tavern most of the day. It was glorious sunshine. Well, we all got a bit stewed as you do, and one of the chaps suggested this party out at Woodstock. So we all piled into Tom's Hummer and went over there."

"Hummer, sir?"

"Oh yes. One of those American things, adapted from some kind of military jeep I believe. They're all the rage in the States. Totally impractical in quaint old Oxfordshire of course. Could hardly fit down some of the lanes. Bloody enormous beast but great fun."

Especially if you are pissed or high on drugs, Cotteril thought. "And you arrived at the party at…?"

"At around eight o'clock; can't be exact I'm afraid, a bit stewed."

"And you stayed until when, sir?"

"The following morning. We crashed out at about three or four in the morning. Everyone was wasted. I woke up at about ten, ten-thirty, something like that."

"And you never left the party all evening?

"No, um, am I under suspicion, Sergeant?"

"Just routine, sir. We have to know where everybody was at the time of your father's death. Sorry, sir, just a few more questions."

Scott had been flicking his eyes above his shoulder at intervals, Cotteril realised there must be either a clock or a mirror there. Suddenly he became very agitated.

"I'm sorry but you see I was expecting someone when you arrived. Could we do this later perhaps?"

"I won't keep you much longer, sir."

The bell rang on its little spring. A youth had sauntered up the driveway as if he owned the street and was now at the door. Cotteril recognised a dealer when he saw one, they have an arrogance all their own. Scott smiled weakly at the sergeant as the bell rang again.

"That may be who you are waiting for, sir," he said, enjoying Scott's obvious discomfort.

"Um, no. No I don't think so. Probably one of Gerri's girlies." A fine line of sweat had broken out on his top lip.

The bell rang again and it sounded as if the person outside was getting impatient. Cotteril heard running feet above him, then a voice. "Scott? It's Melvin. Answer the bloody door, I'm on the phone."

Scott smiled at the sergeant again. "Um, perhaps I'd best

get it. Shan't be a minute." He stood and left the room, closing the door behind him.

Cotteril was on his feet in an instant. He moved to the window nearest the front porch and opened it. The window was quite new and moved smoothly and silently, and it opened considerably wider than he had expected, giving him an idea. Instead of just listening, he stealthily climbed out of the window and stood by the porch, no more than three feet from the caller.

"Look, man, I can't do it now. We've got visitors," Scott explained in hushed tones.

"I don't care nuffin' 'bout no visitors, man. I came all the way up here to deal so let's deal. You got the money?"

"Look, you don't understand. There's someone here. I can't deal. I'll get caught. I'll come to you, later."

But the visitor wasn't having any of it. "Look, man, it took me like an hour to get here. Now you go get the money, I ain't going to be around later. Here's the stuff, now get my money."

That's what Cotteril wanted to hear. He stepped out from behind the porch and in one swift motion grabbed the youth's arm and shoving it hard up his back, slammed him against the brickwork of the porch. "You are under arrest for the possession and distribution of a controlled substance."

"Hey! What? What's going on? Ow! Hey, man, you're breaking my arm." His eyes fell on Scott. "You're dead, man. You hear? Dead!"

"I can add threatening behaviour to the sheet if you like?" Cotteril said, enjoying himself. He had slapped the new style handcuffs on the youth's wrists; with these you have total control over your subject. Holding them by the bar between the cuffs, you can, with a twist of the wrist, have the offender either on his tippy-toes or on the ground. Cotteril chose the ground. He removed his mobile phone and speed-dialled the station. "Send a car up to 23, The Willows. I have a drug dealer under arrest, make it quick." He put the phone away again and, by the twist of his wrist, got the youth to stand again. "Let's go inside shall we?"

During all this Scott stood with his mouth open and was joined very quickly by, Cotteril assumed, Geraldine. Both were unceremoniously pushed aside by Cotteril and the youth coming through the door. He kicked it closed behind him, he may have some pals waiting outside; he was sure he heard the thumping from a "boom box", the monster speakers youths seem to like in the boot of their cars these days. In all probability there was someone in it.

He led them into the lounge and hurled the youth onto the settee and stood over him, menacingly. "Name," he barked.

"Eh? What man? Fuck off, I ain't telling you shit!"

"No matter," Cotteril said. "Caught in possession. Caught distributing. You're going away and good riddance too."

"Fuck off!" the youth spat at Cotteril and tried to kick him.

"Offensive behaviour, attempted assault on a police officer in the pursuit of his duty. It keeps piling up, doesn't it, sonny?" Cotteril pulled out his phone again.

"Cotteril here. Tell the car there's a vehicle outside the property. Apprehend the driver, suspected of carrying drugs." He listened then rang off and replaced the phone in his pocket.

He turned to Scott. "Want to talk about it, Scott?"

"You keep your fucking mouth shut!" the youth screamed. Scott blanched and stepped back in alarm.

"Scott, what's happening?" Geraldine asked, having awakened from wherever it was her brain had been holidaying. "Who is this policeman? Why is he here?"

"Yeah, why's he here, Scott?" the youth spat at him.

"Dirty little bugger, aren't you?" Cotteril said as he heard cars screeching to halt outside. He walked to the window.

"Seems your little friends have been caught napping," he said over his shoulder. "I should come up here more often."

Chapter 9

Greenwold looked up as Cotteril entered the squad room later that afternoon.

"I understand you've had a run in with a local drug dealer, well done."

"Thank you, sir."

"Now, amidst all this excitement, did you get the statements I asked for?"

"I thought it better to bring them in for their statements, as Scott is complicit in the drugs thing, sir."

"Shall we go and see them then?"

As Greenwold and Cotteril entered the room, Scott jumped nervously in his chair.

"You realise you are not under arrest. You are here to help with our inquiries into your father's death," Greenwold explained. "You are free to leave whenever you choose but we may be in touch to follow up on the other matter at a later date." The two men sat opposite Scott who licked his lips nervously. "I'm sorry, would you care for a cup of tea or coffee?"

"Coke?"

"A cola please, Sergeant." Cotteril left the room briefly to ask the constable to get the drink. Greenwold waited until he had sat down again.

"Now. Sergeant Cotteril tells me that you were at an all-night party in Woodstock on the night of your father's demise. Is that true?"

Scott gulped again, his eyes searching the inspector's face. "Yes," he said in a quiet voice.

"Could anyone there corroborate your story?"

"I think so, yeah. We were pretty wast… drunk most of the night but someone is certain to remember me being there. Try Lizzy Haden or Tom Loathe." The sergeant scribbled down the names.

"Do you have addresses for them?"

"You can find them at their rooms at uni."

"Were you very close to your father?"

"Not especially. We got on but didn't socialise if that's what you mean. We skied together a couple of times a year but that was it."

The two officers just sat silently, watching him. He licked his lips again. Greenwold found that silence was like a vacuum; human nature abhors it and has to fill it.

"Dad was always working whenever I came home. I didn't get to see much of him. I wish I had now." He looked down into his lap as his voice tailed off.

"But we heard you talked to your father quite often. In fact," the inspector pulled out a sheet from the folder on the desk and made a meal of reading it, "you spoke to him on the day of the murder, didn't you?"

"Well, yes. I rang him of course but…"

"What for?"

"Sorry?"

"What did you call him for?"

"You know, stuff. To talk."

"To ask for money?"

Scott's mouth fell open. He seemed to shrink in the chair. He took a deep breath. "Yes. I called him to ask him for some cash."

"This was quite a common occurrence wasn't it, sir? You, asking him for money. What was it for?"

"I'm sorry?"

"The money." He looked at the sheet again. "I see your fees were all paid in advance and you were, as you said, living in rooms. That is, on the college grounds. So they were paid for as well. You had a generous allowance toward food et cetera. So what did you need the money for?"

Scott was thunderstruck. His brain had turned to mush. He couldn't think.

Inspector Greenwold leaned forward and spoke in a low, stern voice. "Do you realise, sir, that your father was misappropriating funds from his company to meet your incessant demands on him?" Scott's eyes started to fill up. "What was the money for? It must have been important to drive your father to steal. What was it?"

Scott fell to pieces. Tears stained his face and he sobbed uncontrollably. Inspector Greenwold and Sergeant Cotteril stood and left the room.

Geraldine was completely different. She was happily chatting away to the poor constable on the door, completely oblivious to the fact he wasn't answering or taking the slightest interest in what she was saying. He wouldn't have been able to get a word in anyway. She smiled brightly at the inspector and sergeant as they entered the room; the constable beat a hasty retreat.

"Oh, hello," she gushed. "That was jolly exciting today wasn't it? You were so brave. Apprehending a villain, you were so macho." She actually fluttered her eyelashes at him, Inspector Greenwold thought, my God!

"Miss Prentice…"

"Geraldine or Gerri if you prefer." The inspector ignored her interruption.

"Miss Prentice, we would like to ask you some questions to help in our inquiries into your father's death."

"Ok."

"Where were you on the night in question?"

"I was in Paris. At Le Louvre as it happens. I study eighteenth century art you know. We, the girls and I, went at around seven o'clock French time, and then on to one of those pavement restaurants nearby. Can't remember exactly which one. The girls will vouch for me."

"Thank you, perhaps you would leave their names and contact details with the sergeant before you leave?"

"Ok."

"When was the last time you spoke to your father?"

"Do you know, I've been trying to remember ever since I heard what happened. I think it was the week before, on Tuesday. I called him at work to sort out some silly misunderstanding. He seemed ok then." She beamed at the men.

"What misunderstanding, miss?"

"Oh, over a bill or something to do with the hotel, I can't remember exactly. Why? Is it important?"

It was to your father, you spoiled brat, the inspector thought but said, "Not really, miss. Just trying to put your father's last few days together. What he did, how he felt, if there was anything on his mind. Just routine." Nothing, the inspector thought. She feels nothing about this. Her father's dead and she's treating it like a field trip. I'd like to slap her stupid face. He and Cotteril exchanged glances, she smiled on.

"I'm sorry, miss, but I'm not sure you have grasped what has happened here."

"Sorry?"

"Your father was murdered on his way home last week. Does that mean nothing to you? Are you not sad?"

"Oh yes, I'm sad. I was very sad when Mumsie rang and told me what happened and I had to come home, and I was having such fun over there…" she tailed off as if it was a huge inconvenience that her father had chosen to get killed while she was "having fun". And "Mumsie"? Who the hell

51

says "Mumsie" these days? That belongs to Miss Marple's era, not now.

"Have you heard the name David or Dave Quinn?"

"No."

"You didn't think very long."

"Well I don't, know the name that is."

"Did you know that man who was arrested today at your house?"

She brightened up again and stared with hero worship at Sergeant Cotteril. "Yes, he was one of Scotty's friends.They're all incredibly boring, just want to drink and take drugs all the time."

"Thank you, miss. That will be all for now."

"Ok."

In reception, Mrs Prentice and Mr MacAllistair were anxiously waiting. As Geraldine entered they both leapt to their feet. Mrs Prentice rushed to her daughter and enfolded her in her arms, glaring at Inspector Greenwold.

"What did you have to bring her here for?" she snarled. "Couldn't you talk to her at home?"

"In view of what had occurred…"

"What has that to do with anything?" she snapped. "That's nothing to do with Gerri; talk to Scott, but leave Gerri out of it." All the time she was snapping and snarling at the inspector, MacAllistair was trying to placate her, trying to clam her down. You're welcome to her, mate, Cotteril thought.

"Madam, we are trying to investigate a murder…"

"Well you should get on with that then and leave her out of it."

"We had to establish Miss Prentice's whereabouts at the time…"

"I *told* you. She was in Paris. Nowhere near Perry Green. Come on, darling, we're going home now." She glared, "And don't you dare try to stop us," at the policemen.

"Charming family," Inspector Greenwold said as the door swung shut.

Chapter 10

The newly set up incident room thronged with activity. Spirits were high. There was a general consensus of "we're getting there" fuelling speculations amongst the assembled best that Perry Green had to offer. As usual Inspector Greenwold had to clap his hands to attract attention and calm the growing volume.

"So, how are we doing?" he said by way of introduction. At this point he was aware that someone else had joined the clan who had not been there on previous occasions - the superintendent. He glanced at him, standing in his nice, shiny uniform by the door and got a nod of approval to continue.

"Ok, what can you tell me about victim number two, Mr Quinn?" He tapped the photograph taken by the pathologist that had been taped to the white board.

"I found his ex-wife living down in Poole in Dorset with her 'partner'." Constable Moore said.

"Yes?"

"She appears to have changed sides, sir."

"Go on."

"She is living, very happily apparently, with a Miss Eileen Church and has no intention to take Mr Quinn for any of his money. She just wants out of the relationship and marriage to pursue her 'true sexuality', sir." A few sniggers were heard around the room. "That's what she said, sir."

"Her whereabouts on the night in question?"

"Serving dinners at the restaurant she runs with her partner. Lots of witnesses including a JP and a cabinet minister."

"You should have left out the last one, it didn't add to the authenticity."

Laughter all around now, the superintendent snorted and left the room. "Ok, so Mrs Quinn is out of the picture. And I assume the divorce was amicable?"

"Apart from him not wanting it, yes sir. She was quite happy with the way things went and wants nothing from his estate. She was upset to hear what had happened but, in my opinion, not ready to jump in and grab what she could.

"I took the liberty of finding out if there was a will, sir. There was, lodged with their solicitor just after the divorce, it cut her out of everything. All of his estate goes to his brother in Wales."

"And do we know the whereabouts of this brother?"

"Yes, sir, he's up to his armpits in sheep in Lampeter, mid Wales. He had no idea he had been named in the will and hadn't seen his brother for ten years. They weren't close, they had different fathers and are a generation apart, sir."

"Thank you. Has anyone turned up a link between the two victims?" A general shaking of heads met his gaze. "Keep looking, there must be something. Who was looking into Quinn's past?" A hand went up in the middle of the room belonging to WPC Allen.

"Yes?"

"Nothing there, sir. He spent until the last five years in his hometown of Northampton. Mr Prentice came from London."

"Ok, but there has to be a link somewhere. Keep digging. Back here at o-nine-hundred tomorrow please. Thank you."

He turned to Sergeant Cotteril, "Let's see if Mrs Prentice has calmed down shall we?"

"Should we take protective clothing?"

"Quite probably."

A WPC was waiting outside the squad room for the inspector. "Would you pop in and see the pathologist before you go, sir? He said it was important."

Greenwold and Cotteril exchanged glances; maybe there had been a break-through. "Thank you, Constable, we will go there directly."

Colin was at his computer typing up a report when they entered his domain.

"We got your message, Colin," Inspector Greenwold said.

"Ah yes. I don't know if it will help or not but in the interests of keeping you abreast of all we find…" He stood and walked through to the mortuary. He opened one of the doors and slid the gurney out. "Mr Quinn caught my attention," he said. "I understand he was estranged from his wife?"

"Yes. More than you know."

"Oh?"

"She has discovered she is gay." Cotteril supplied.

"Oh! Then this may be of interest to you. It appears our Mr Quinn had had intercourse very shortly before his demise. I found female DNA on his genitals."

"So he wasn't wearing a condom?" Cotteril hazarded.

"Correct, Sergeant." He covered the corpse again and slid the gurney back.

"Thanks, Colin, good work," Greenwold said appreciatively.

As they left the mortuary he turned to Cotteril, "I'll talk to Mrs Prentice again while you go to the Kings Arms and find out who the mystery woman is."

*

Greenwold was not surprised when MacAllistair opened the door.

"Inspector," he said, taken aback. "Do come in." He stood aside to allow him past. "We're in the sitting room." He led the way to where the Prentice family were assembled. Scott in particular sat up straight at the inspector's entrance; Gerri gave him the briefest of glances and Mrs Prentice, to her credit, looked guilty. She stood and ushered the inspector to a seat.

"How can we help, Inspector?" she asked with every sign of being sincere. "I am sorry for my outburst at the station. Please accept my apology."

"Of course, Mrs Prentice. Think no more of it. Sorry to interrupt you at this time but we still need your statement."

She put her hand to her mouth, "Oh, Inspector, I am so sorry. I forgot all about it. Yes, let's get it done now. Would you come through to the dining room, we'll have more privacy there."

She led him through a door into a room of similar dimensions to the lounge with a large mahogany table and chairs. A matching sideboard was against one wall and the room was bathed in subtle lighting.

"Please sit down." She indicated a chair opposite from herself. They sat and Greenwold produced a statement form.

"Now, could we start with the night in question. You had retired to bed at what time?"

"Eleven o'clock, I watched *Newsnight* then went straight up."

"And you were expecting Mr Prentice at what time?"

"I never knew what time he would be home. He was either working late, or had to go to town or… Well Larry tells me you know now, he often went to his 'lover' before coming home to his wife."

"And your sleeping arrangements?"

"Yes, that must seem strange. Do you and your wife still share the marital bed, Inspector?"

"Yes. We wouldn't think of being apart."

"Lucky you. Brian announced some years ago that he would move into the second bedroom. His reason being that he didn't want to disturb me by arriving home late at night, and his snoring often awakened me.

"At the time I was feeling very lethargic during the day, I found out later I was acutely anaemic. So I took his suggestion as concern for my getting a good night's sleep and I appreciated it. But when I suggested we return to the status quo as it were, he wasn't interested. That hurt, Inspector."

"Were you expecting him home that night?"

"Yes. He had said nothing to the contrary. But I often don't hear him arrive home. He can be very quiet, partially out of consideration for me."

"When would you normally see him if he didn't get back until after you had retired for the night?"

"At breakfast in the morning. At around eight o'clock.

"I usually get up and cook breakfast while he gets ready for work. We eat together then he leaves."

"Please don't take offence at my next question, it is purely routine that I ask but, did you and Mr Prentice have any financial concerns?"

"Apart from having children who are monetary black holes you mean? No, I don't think so. Brian handles all that, I have a card I use for shopping and anything else I need and the bill is always paid in full at the end of the month." She smiled amiably.

"Do you own this house? Do you have a mortgage?"

"The mortgage was paid off years ago. We went through hell to pay it off as quickly as possible before the children were born. Well, actually Scott was three when we paid the final instalment. So the house is ours, lock, stock and barrel."

"You may think this next question impertinent, Mrs Prentice, but please bear with me. What do you do with your day?"

She laughed, throwing her head back. "Sorry, Inspector, Brian used to ask the very same question.

"I do housework. It's not easy keeping a house this size clean and tidy even after the children left. I meet with friends in town most afternoons. I have the Oxfam shop I work in twice a week, and two evenings a week I go to keep-fit at the sports centre.

"I keep busy, Inspector, my days – or evenings for that matter – are never dull."

"Well thank you, Mrs Prentice, I hope this hasn't been too much of an ordeal for you."

"Not at all, Inspector."

Having read the statement back, Mrs Prentice signed it and he bade everyone good night and left.

Chapter 11

As Sergeant Cotteril made his way to the bar, he acknowledged the faces he usually saw there. George and Tom, the old-timers forever rooted to the table under the dartboard, Sally and Dave behind the bar. The raucous laughter of Molly: a woman with the sensitivity of a docker, and Steeley the local dope fiend who made himself scarce as soon as he saw Cotteril come through the door.

"Hello Paul, not your night is it?" Sally asked as she pulled him a pint of bitter.

"No, I'm here on business tonight, Sally."

"So you don't want this then?"

"Best not to waste it," he said, handing over the money and taking the pint.

As she gave him his change he leant across the bar to her and lowered his voice. "Sally, do you know a man called Dave Quinn? About five-eight, medium build, black hair going grey at the temples?"

"Dave? Yeah, he comes in here most nights on his way home from work. Come to think of it I haven't seen him for a few nights now. Why? What's he done?"

"Him? He hasn't done anything." Except get himself killed, he thought. "Does he have a lady friend at all? Someone he meets here?"

Sally laughed. "You mean Cheryl. She's sweet on him, lord knows why."

"Why do you say that?"

"He's still hung up on that bitch who ran off and left him. His wife."

"Actually he's divorced."

"What? He always told us he would never divorce her. Are you sure?" Cotteril just nodded. "The little git," Sally said uncharitably. "It'd break poor Cheryl's heart if she knew."

That's not all it'd break if she knew the entire story, Cotteril thought, but kept his own counsel.

"Is she in tonight?" he asked.

"Follow my eyes," she said and turned to look at the far end of the bar where a plump woman in her late twenties sat on a bar stool sipping at a long drink.

"Thanks, Sally," he said out of the corner of his mouth.

He made his way to the woman, trying not to attract attention, but she had spotted him almost immediately and hadn't taken her eyes off him as he approached. The smile that started out whimsical was as bright as the sunlight by the time he reached her.

"Hello," she said, breathless. She put her glass on the bar and turned to face him fully. She was quite attractive in a mumsie sort of way. She had a generous smile with full, red lips and beautiful white teeth. She had buxom proportions that she liked to display, but not tartily. He could see why Quinn would be attracted to her.

"Cheryl?"

She looked at him askance, "Yes? How did you know my name?"

He took his warrant card from his pocket and showed it to her carefully, "DS Cotteril, Perry Green CID," he said, putting it away again. She snorted down her nose and turned back to the bar and her drink.

"Well if you think I'm one of them, you're mistaken. I'm waiting for someone."

"I know," he said, assuming "one of them" was a lady of easy virtue. "He won't be coming." She looked at him inquiringly. "Can we go somewhere private?"

"What for?"

"I need to talk to you about David Quinn."

After a pause she said, "Over here," and led him to a table in the corner, out of anyone's gaze. They sat down and leaned in close.

"I'm sorry to have to tell you that Dave has passed away." Well, he thought, it sounds better than "was butchered by a knife wielding maniac" but, on the face of it, it wouldn't have mattered. Her head shot back, eyes wide and filled immediately with tears. She searched in her handbag for a handkerchief.

"What...? What happened?" she asked after pulling herself together.

"I'm afraid he was murdered."

"No!" she started. "Who? Who would want to do that to Dave?"

"That's what we are trying to find out, Cheryl. Would you mind coming down to the station to give a statement?" She shook her head. "Finish your drink," he said and took his own advice.

Once in the interview room, the tears came. Cotteril waited patiently for a full half-hour before she was able to talk clearly.

"How long have you known Mr Quinn?"

She thought a moment, "About five or six weeks."

"Do you know a Brian Prentice?"

She looked puzzled. "No. Why?"

Damn, he thought, worth a try though. "Cheryl, could you tell me the nature of your relationship with Mr Quinn?"

"We were friends, very good friends. He was going to leave his wife to be with me. He said he would get a divorce if he could find her but she had run off with someone and he didn't know where she had gone."

He let it pass, "Did you have a physical relationship with him?"

"I beg your pardon?"

"I'm sorry but I have to ask this. Did you?"

"Well, we're both healthy, normal, human beings. Of course it developed into a physical relationship. Why wouldn't it?"

"No reason, no reason at all. On Tuesday, this Tuesday, did you meet with him?"

She nodded, her big eyes on the sergeant. It was like being looked at by one of those puppy dogs with big, brown eyes. It made you want to go "Ahhh."

"Cheryl, I'm sorry to have to ask but did you have intercourse with him on that occasion?" She bit her lip and nodded. "Thank you. Was this at his flat?"

"No. We were supposed to have met at the pub when he finished work, but I got held up so I said we would make it another night." Cotteril nodded encouragingly. "Well, as it happens I got away earlier than I expected so I thought it would be a nice surprise if I met him at his home."

"Did you go there often?"

"Not really, only a few times."

"Go on."

"Well, as I was crossing the garages he pulled in. He had had a few at the Indian on his way home and was…" she paused and blushed coyly. "He was in a playful mood."

"Yes?"

"Do I have to go into details?"

"Please don't leave anything out, something inconsequential to you may have some bearing on the circumstances of his death."

"Well, as I said, he was a little tipsy and playful so instead of going up to his flat we, sort of, you know, in the car." She was a deep red now, but there was a smile playing about her lips.

"You had intercourse in the back of his car," Cotteril paraphrased.

"Yes." Then she started crying again. "I'm sorry," she said. "It's just that, it was the last time…"

"It's ok," he said gently.

"What happened?" she asked in a small voice.

"After you left he was attacked and killed. What time did you leave him?"

She shook her head. "Sorry, she said. "I don't know. It wasn't long after, you know."

"Did you see or hear anything as you left?"

"No."

"Did you go back to his flat after…?"

"No. No he said he had to get up early. He offered to drive me home but I told him not be silly. Anyway, I enjoy the walk. So we put the car away…" she stopped, a look of recollection on her face. "There was another car. It pulled up… Oh, but that was a taxi turning round. Yes, a taxi turned round in the garages just as I left him."

"Did you see what taxi company it was?" Cotteril asked, but she was already crying. Crying fit to bust. The intensity of her grief got to him. He fetched a WPC to take her to the canteen for a cup of hot, sweet tea.

Still no nearer, he thought. What on earth is the connection between these two?

Chapter 12

Inspector Greenwold was the last to arrive in the incident room the next morning but he got straight on with business.

"Ok, people, let's have it. What have you got for me? Sergeant, what of Mr Quinn?"

"He's been seeing a Miss Cheryl Betteridge. He met her in the Kings Arms fairly regularly. She was under the impression he was still married and trying to find Mrs Quinn to seek a divorce." A ripple of laughter from the men and "poor cow" from the WPCs passed around the room. "They had been having a relationship for some weeks and…"

The desk sergeant coming into the room and speaking into Inspector Greenwold's ear interrupted him. The Inspector stared at the officer, "Is that what he said?"

"Yes, sir. Exactly, sir."

He turned to the room again, a serious look on his face. "There may have been another one." A groan rose from the assembled. "A young girl this time, in the car park at Asda. Same MO, Colin thinks." He turned to Cotteril, "Sergeant, if you would come with me, the rest of you carry on until I confirm that the body count is now three."

The car park at Asda was cordoned off and a white tent covered a small area to the rear. Inside, suited in white again, Inspector Greenwold and Sergeant Cotteril looked down on the body of a young girl, dressed in "going out" clothes. Her long red hair covered half her face and the hilt of a knife protruded from the mauve glitter boob tube she was wearing.

"Must've been coming home from Bohemia," Cotteril said sadly. "Can't be more than eighteen." He shook his head.

"Life was extinct at approximately one-thirty this morning," Colin said. "Looks like the same MO, a single blow with an ordinary kitchen knife. No signs of a struggle. She bled out but was probably unconscious from the blow.

"This time the body was as you see it. On her back."

A WPC sniffed into her handkerchief at the entrance to the tent. Inspector Greenwold put a kindly hand on her shoulder. "Off you go, Shirley, back to the station. Get a cup of tea."

"I think I know her, sir," she sniffed. "I think it's Emily Patterson, she lives just over there," she pointed, forgetting they were in a tent.

"Do you know her address?"

"Wood Green Road, I don't know what number but I know which house it is, I've seen her coming and going. I live just down the road."

"Show the sergeant which house it is, then get yourself off to the station… And that's an order, Constable."

"Thank you, sir. Sorry, sir."

"For what? For feeling? For being human? There's worse things, Constable, much worse. Get along now."

He turned his attention back to the body. "What possible connection has she got to the other two?" he said mostly to himself. He looked at Colin, "Except that she's dead by the same hand."

"We don't know that for certain yet, but it certainly looks that way. I'll have a report to you as soon as possible, Joe. This bastard has to be stopped, and soon."

Outside the tent, Joe Greenwold took a breath of morning air. He looked around; the alleyway leading to the front of the

Bohemia nightclub was just ten yards away. She had, in all probability, come along that alleyway. Why wait until she's out here in the car park? The cover of dark in the alley would surely be better for the assailant. He turned to Colin as he stepped out of the tent. "Was the body moved at all?"

Colin shook his head, "No, no chance of that. The blood is contained underneath her and just around where she lay." He sniffed loudly. "She fell where she was struck."

"Have the boys cordon off that alley and go over it with a fine-toothed comb."

Colin looked at the alleyway, "You think the assailant waited there?"

"Possibly, no chance of being seen no matter how long he'd have to wait."

"Why wait until the poor girl was out here then?"

"More importantly, why wasn't the body discovered by other people leaving the club?" They both looked up at the lampposts nearby, the glass was smashed in the one nearest to them but one across the other side caught Greenwold's attention. "There's a CCTV on that one. Where would it be operated from?" He called to a constable who was carrying an empty body bag to the tent.

The man trotted over to him. "Sir?"

"Find out where that CCTV is operated from. Do it and do it now. If there's any tapes I want them, understand? No one gets in your way - you have my full authority. Now go!"

The constable dropped the bag and ran back the way he had come. Greenwold walked over to the camera and looked back at the scene. Yes, he thought, it might just be in view. We need a break. We need something to do instead of just waiting for the next body to turn up.

Twenty minutes later the constable appeared again and looked around. "Over here," Greenwold shouted. He ran up and, slightly out of breath said, "It's Asda's security, sir. I have a man opening up now if you would like to come with me."

"Good man, lead the way."

In the security room, a guard who looked like he had just fallen out of bed was rewinding a videocassette. He looked up at Greenwold's arrival.

"Should have it for you in a minute or two," he said. "Who was it?" he nodded to the door.

"We're not certain yet, a young girl."

"Probably from Bohemia, they cut across here most nights to go home. They used to take the trolleys and break the windows until we chained them up and put up these cameras."

"*These cameras*? There's more than one?"

"Yeah, there's three."

"Show me where they are. Constable, when that's finished rewinding take it to the station, to Warren." He turned and marched out of the room following the guard.

The other two cameras had been situated at the far end of the car park and at the front of the store. There was no chance of either of them picking anything up; it all depended on that one tape now.

They sat in a small room, surrounded by monitors and various pieces of electric and electronic hardware. Warren, who ran the AV lab at the station, was a member of the ever-growing forensic team. If there were anything to be had from the tape, he would find it.

"It's quite dark as it's at the extent of the camera's range, but there's something there," he said, staring intently at the screen. "I'll put it through some software we have and see if I can enhance it." He ejected the cassette from the recorder and disappeared out of the room.

Greenwold stood, not certain what to do next. He had been totally focussed on that tape and now Warren had taken it to weave his magic on it he was lost. Finally he went back up to the incident room and the white board.

More facts were being added and, of course, pictures of the latest victim.

Just a child, he thought sullenly. He pulled a chair over and sat studying the board. We have so much information but, at the moment, that was only causing more questions to arise.

Three murders in quick succession: in different places and at different times of the day. The victims were of different social status and different ages.

What do they have in common? What am I not seeing?

They live far apart. They don't seem to frequent the same places - or do they? He filed that away for an action at the next briefing. Where's the rhyme, the reason?

There are no clues at the scene - that's something I thought every killer left, some trace of being at the scene, but somehow this one doesn't, why?

He heard a polite cough from behind. "Yes, Sergeant?" he said without looking round.

"Just come back from seeing the girl's parents, sir."

Greenwold stood and faced him. "I'm sorry," he said in a gentle voice. "How was it? It's not a nice thing to have to do."

"Understandably they're totally destroyed by the news. They had only reported her missing an hour before I arrived. They thought it was good that I was there so quickly."

"Let's go and sit down somewhere." Cotteril looked over the inspector's shoulder, an anxious expression on his face. "They'll find us when there's something to see, come on." He led him to the canteen where they sat in the corner away from everyone else.

"Did they have much to say?" he asked hopefully. Cotteril shook his head. "No, silly of me. Of course not."

"She seemed a lovely girl, sir. Doing well at school, helpful to her parents. Good at sports. They said she wanted to go to university, she was tipped to do well at her A levels." He lapsed into silence. "Such a waste," he said quietly.

WPC Brooks, who he had sent away from the scene, came to get them. "Warren's got something, sir."

They almost ran to the AV room. Many of the officers from the incident room were already there and in the middle of it all was a desk strewn with bits and pieces of technology, and in the centre, a large very high definition TV Monitor. The room was in darkness apart from the screen.

"Give me some good news, Warren," the inspector said breathlessly as he seated himself alongside the technician.

"We've got the murder on tape, sir. I'm just cueing it up." The room fell silent as they watched the screen.

They saw various boys and girls coming from the alleyway across the car park. Some laughing. Some arguing. Some being sick and staggering. Then, after a pause, the victim stepped out of the alley. She went a few yards then stopped as if she heard something behind her. A figure stepped out of the alley, walked up to her and…

Everyone in the room gasped as the blade went in. Behind them the door banged as someone rushed out. Everybody else's attention was on the screen, unable to take in what they had just seen.

The action of the killer was so positive, so decisive. No messing, straight up to the girl and bang. So hard the girl fell backwards and apart from moving her hands to the knife, made no motion. The killer watched the victim until sure she was dead, then looked around and disappeared back into the alleyway. All that was left on the screen was the dead girl lying in the half shadows.

After a pause, the room exploded into action.

"Rewind," ordered Greenwold over the noise of the others behind him. "People," he shouted. "People. I want every one of you to study the killer in every detail. I want every one of you to be able to recognise the killer by their slightest movement. We *have* to find this person before he strikes again. Warren?"

The tape ran again. Warren was able to stop it and move it forward and backwards with great accuracy and no loss of video quality. The figure was dressed entirely in black. Tight fitting jacket or top, tight trousers, black trainers, gloves and ski mask.

Colin joined the throng on the third showing and immediately chimed in, "No wonder there were no forensics." Everyone looked him and waited for the revelation.

"He was wearing something like leatherette, or a supple plastic. There's nothing that can be left behind from a material like that. I'll bet the shoes, gloves and hood are of a similar material. And the knife action... A thrust. It's so unusual, almost as if whoever it is hasn't been shown how to use a knife properly. Or it's a technique they have developed for expediency. It certainly works."

"Well one thing is certain," Greenwold added, "he didn't walk there dressed like that. He must have a car nearby or got changed in the alleyway. I want that alley dusted. I want it gone over until we've worn it down to the rubble underneath. Colin, I want you to study this footage and anything you see, anything at all, no matter how wild you think it is. I want to know, got that?"

"Sure, Joe, but I have to perform the autopsy on the poor girl first." The room suddenly fell silent. In their excitement they had forgotten the girl lying on the slab.

"Of course," Greenwold patted Colin's shoulder.

Chapter 13

Back in the incident room, Sergeant Cotteril jumped to his feet as Greenwold walked in. "Sorry, sir, I couldn't watch any more. Not having met the girl's parents and seen where she lived…"

"It's ok, Sergeant, but now we need to find out everything we can about her. For starters, what's her name?"

"Emily. Emily Patterson, sir. WPC Brooks was right about that. She had just turned eighteen, it was only the third time she had gone to the Bohemia club."

"Did she go alone? Didn't she go with some friends?"

"She went with two other girls: Penny Abrahams and Collette Jones, both from the same school, both eighteen."

"So why didn't she leave with them? Were they still inside when it happened or had they left earlier?"

"They were probably still inside, sir. Emily had to be home at one-thirty but the others could stay out longer. She often complained to her parents about them being too strict with her. They're blaming themselves, sir."

"Ok, we need to talk to these girls to find out if Emily left with anyone, a boy maybe? We also need to talk to the bouncers at the club. They may have seen someone hanging around or remember someone going into the alleyway after Emily. Do we have a good photo of her?"

"Here, sir. She's wearing almost the same clothes as she had on last night." He handed Greenwold a picture that had obviously been printed off a computer. He looked at it for a long while then handed it back to Cotteril.

"You take the club; I'll go to the girl's school. Which one was it?"

"Eversholt School, sir."

Greenwold looked around. "WPC Betteridge."

The constable looked round, "Yes, sir?"

"You're coming with me. I have to interview two teenage girls and I need a chaperone and someone who is nearer their age to act as interpreter. Get your coat and meet me in reception in ten minutes."

"Yes, sir."

Before he left he went back to the AV room where Warren and Colin were still poring over the footage.

"Anything new?"

"We think he's wearing either dark brown or blue. It certainly isn't black," Warren said, without taking his eyes off the screen.

"How can you tell?"

"It's the way the colour blends into the darkness around him. Darkness isn't black, it's dark shades, an amalgam of colours. A black outfit could be seen in dark shadows as a slightly darker area. Brown or blue would blend much better."

"Fascinating. Whoever it is, they've certainly worked at it. The material, the colour and the location for the crime: very fastidious." He stood looking over their shoulders at the poor girl living the last few seconds of her life over and over again. "Let me know immediately you spot anything else, Warren. Aren't you supposed to be carrying out an autopsy, Colin?"

"Quite right, Joe. I'll be back, Warren, keep my seat warm."

They walked side by side, each with their own thoughts. "We're going to get this bastard," Greenwold said with venom. "And I hope he doesn't want to come quietly."

"I'll pretend I didn't hear that, Joe."

Eversholt School for Young Ladies, to give the institute its full name, is a self-governing school that has very high standards for its pupils. Inspector Greenwold had heard that competition was fierce between parents vying to get their "little princess" a place there.

At the front door they were met by a cheerful young lady, who led them to the principal's office. They were asked to wait outside and sat on hard chairs like two naughty children sent for the "book and cane" as in Greenwold's day.

Eventually the door opened and a tall, stocky woman strode out, hand outstretched to greet them.

"Cybil Harmsworth, principal of Eversholt School for Young Ladies," she announced.

"Detective Inspector Greenwold and Woman Police Constable Betteridge."

"Do come in. Now what can I do for you, Detective Inspector?"

"This is of a sensitive nature, Mrs Harmsworth."

"Miss," she corrected.

I'm not surprised, Betteridge thought.

"Miss. We are investigating a very serious crime that took place in the very early hours of this morning. I believe you have a student here, an Emily Patterson?"

She nodded. "An excellent scholar, we have high hopes for her. I do hope she is not in trouble."

"I'm sorry to have to tell you, Miss Harmsworth, that Emily was found this morning in the car park at Asda. She had been stabbed to death."

The blood drained from her face. She froze, unable to move. Then she slowly turned her head to look at a crucifix hanging on the wall. She seemed to get some strength from that as some of her colour came back, along with her voice.

"I really do not know what to say. She was such a lovely girl with a wonderful disposition. I do hope her parents are being comforted?"

"Rest assured we are providing all the support they will need.

"Emily was out last night with two more of your students before the tragedy. I would like to interview them as part of our inquiry. They are," he consulted his notepad, "Penny Abrahams and Collette Jones." She nodded, recognising the names.

"May I use an office to talk to them? WPC Betteridge will be on-hand at all times."

"But of course, however I do believe their parents should be with them during the interview. I could contact them and have them here sometime this afternoon for you."

"I understand your concern, Miss Harmsworth, but time is of the essence. We have a trail that is getting colder by the minute. Both girls are over eighteen and therefore do not, by law, need chaperoning. However, I would be happy for you to sit in. We will be seeing both of them together."

Miss Harmsworth thought about it, torn between her civic duty and the threat of a lawsuit from the parents. Finally she agreed.

The girls were shown into the principal's office and were startled to see the police officers sitting behind the desk. They looked anxiously at one another and drew closer together for support. Miss Harmsworth stood at the door.

"Thank you for coming, girls. Firstly I want to reassure you, you have done nothing wrong to my knowledge. We are not here to trick you or make you admit to anything." They looked relived and sat down on the chairs in front of the desk, still close together.

"I am Inspector Greenwold and this is WPC Betteridge. Could I ask your names?"

"Penny Abrahams," the one on the left said.

"Collette Jones," the other, taller girl answered.

"Thank you. I understand you were at the Bohemia night-club last night." They nodded in unison. "At what time did you leave?"

They looked at one another. "At two o'clock this morning," Penny answered.

He could see the expression on Miss Harmsworth's face.

"That's fine, you are both over eighteen and entitled to stay there as long as you like." This was more for Miss Harmsworth than to reassure the girls. He was telling her to lay off them. "You were there with another girl, Emily Patterson?"

They nodded again. Penny spoke up again, "She left before us, at half-past one. She has to be home at that time."

"Is she in trouble? Didn't she get home on time?" Collette asked.

"No, she's not in trouble. Did she leave with anyone, a boy maybe?"

They looked horrified, as if he said had she left with an axe-wielding maniac. Again the shaking heads.

"She went home alone. It isn't far."

"It's only across the road," Collette added.

"And you didn't see anyone follow her out of the club?"

"No. We walked to the door with her and waved her off," Penny said. Collette nodded in agreement.

The inspector sat back, "Thank you, ladies. You have been very helpful."

"Can we go now?" Collette asked.

"Yes, you can go. Thank you again."

After they had left the room, Inspector Greenwold gave Miss Harmsworth her chair back. "I would appreciate it if you keep Emily's death to yourself, Miss Harmsworth. Her parents are struggling to cope and we don't want a panic running through the school do we?"

Her eyes widened at the thought of it, no wonder he hadn't said anything to the girls. "No, Inspector, I expect they will find out soon enough through the press."

"Well thank you for your hospitality, we must be going now. Goodbye."

"Goodbye, Inspector, and er, goodbye." She didn't seem to know how to address WPC Betteridge.

In the car Greenwold asked, "What did you think of them?"

"They were telling the truth, sir."

"Are you sure?"

"You had told them what they were *not* in trouble for, but not what they *were* in trouble for. Very sneaky."

Greenwold smiled, "I can see there's no pulling the wool over your eyes, Constable."

Chapter 14

The Bohemia Club was Perry Green's one and only nightspot for the young and not so young alike. It was open seven nights a week, dividing the week for the different age groups they catered for. It also opened lunchtimes as somewhere to have a beer and listen to music.

It had been run by a number of owners since its first opening, but was always "The Bohemia" in some shape or form. These days it was run by Peter Dickinson, a self-made man - and in Cotteril's opinion it was good of him to take the blame. Dickinson thought he was a younger Peter Stringfellow but he lacked the charm. He surrounded himself with a bevy of beauties that, close up, proved to be just as phoney as the man himself.

Cotteril was ushered into an office, Dickenson was sat behind a desk trying to look important. I must find out how he got his money some time, Cotteril thought as the man stood, a wide grin on his face and his hand outstretched.

"Sergeant. Welcome to my humble establishment. What can I do for you? Are you looking for a venue for the Policeman's Ball?" A rumble from behind Cotteril told him that his bouncer thought his boss was a riot.

He just smiled benignly and sat in the proffered chair. "I'm afraid not. It's on a more serious matter that I hope you can help."

The smile stayed painted on his face. "Oh? What's that then?"

"At one-thirty this morning a young girl, Emily Patterson, was murdered in Asda's car park at the other end of the alley from this club."

"No!" Dickinson said and blew out his cheeks.

"She had been here with a couple of her friends but left early to make her way home to Wood Green Road," Cotteril continued. "We wondered if your men on the door may have seen someone follow her into the alley. Who was on the door this morning?"

"I'm not altogether sure, officer. Harry, get the book will you?" He sat back shaking his head. "Terrible, terrible! And that it should happen in a nice quiet place like Perry Green eh?" They waited in silence until Harry returned with a leather-bound A5 book.

"We, as no doubt you know, officer, keep a book on who we employ and on what nights. We, for our own use, also record in what capacity we employ them. Doorman, bar-staff, dance-floor security, general dogs-body - you get the idea." Cotteril nodded. "Let's see," he said, running his finger down the page. "Ah yes." He stood and went to a wood-fronted filing cabinet and slid out the second drawer. Reaching in, he retracted a file that he flicked though as he returned to his chair.

"It was Paul Maton and Danny Johnson last night on door duty." He handed over the file. "Their addresses are in there; although you would be better off going to Laker's the builders merchants. They moonlight here to supplement their pay."

"Cash in hand?" asked Cotteril, already knowing the answer.

Dickinson spread his hands in a conciliatory manner. "We do everything through the books here, officer. Otherwise we would have the Inland Revenue breathing down our necks, not to mention the VAT man and, no doubt, your good self."

"Thank you for the information," Cotteril said as he stood to leave.

"You're welcome, anything to help the boys in blue eh? Just let us have the file back when you're finished with it, it has their personnel records in it." He gave Cotteril a knowing wink. Cotteril looked at the file in his hand, and the penny dropped. It would have their full employment record and notes of convictions in it, if they had any.

"Thank you, we'll get it back to you as soon as possible."

Laker's wasn't far from the club. As Cotteril parked up to the makeshift offices that had been there as far back as he could remember, a man stepped out of the door wearing a yellow hard-hat. He recognised him as Jerry, the second generation Laker to run the business. He shouted something back through the door before approaching Cotteril's car.

"Officer. How nice to see you. What brings you here?"

"Hello, Jerry, have you got a couple of guys called Paul Maton and Danny Johnson working here today?"

He looked surprised. "Yes. Danny's on the forklift and Paul's in the office. What have they done?"

"Nothing as far as I know. I just need a word."

He shrugged. "Fine. Use the office. Just don't keep them too long eh?"

"I'll be as quick as I can, thanks."

"You go on in. I'll send Danny over." He trudged off leaving the sergeant to let himself into the office.

Paul was making a mug of tea from a battered metal kettle. He turned on hearing the door open and gently set the kettle down on the cabinet.

"Yeah?"

"Paul Maton?"

"Yeah?"

"Sergeant Cotteril, Perry Green CID." He held up his card. "I've ok'd it with Jerry to talk to you. I just want to ask you about last night, or rather, this morning at the Bohemia. You were working there?"

"Yeah, that's right, me and Danny. Why, what's happened?"

Cotteril took a copy of the photograph of Emily from his pocket and handed it to Paul. "Do you remember seeing her there? She came with two others but left alone." He was already nodding his head before Cotteril had finished. A smile broke on his face.

"Yeah I remember her. A little spitfire. We asked her for some ID with her age on. She went off on one because we hadn't asked her mates." He handed the photo back. "Why? She complaining or something? It was all recorded in the book."

"You record everyone you ID?"

"No. Just everyone who says they're going to complain to the management. They never do, even if they don't get in."

"Do you remember her leaving? It would have been around one-thirty."

"Yeah, her two mates waved her off. Then they tried to chat Danny up," he laughed. "Danny's kids are nearly as old as them."

Just then the man himself came into the office. "Jerry said you wanted to talk to me?"

"Yes. I've just been asking Paul here about a girl, Emily Patterson, that was at the club last night." Again, he handed the picture over.

Danny's face broke into a grin. "Oh yeah, I remember her. One of her mates tried to chat me up, it made my day," he laughed. "Mind you, she was probably pissed." He handed it back. "Why, what's up?"

"After leaving the club she walked up the alley to Asda's car park. Do you remember seeing anyone following her? Maybe someone came out of the club after her and went the same way?"

He shook his head slowly, a thoughtful expression on his face. "Not as I recall. I don't think so. Can't be sure of course." He looked at Paul who also shook his head.

"Why don't you get the video from the club?"

"Pardon?"

"The videotape. There's a camera just above the door. It's there to sort out any accusations of us being heavy-handed. They keep the tapes in the back."

"Why didn't Dickinson make me aware of this?" Cotteril said, more to himself than anything.

"Don't ask me. Probably wanted a look for himself first. Cover his arse sort of thing."

"But you don't remember anyone following her out?" Both men shook their heads again. "No, sorry."

"Well, thanks for your time. You've been very helpful."

"Wait a minute," Danny said as he turned to go. "What's this all about? Didn't she get home?"

Cotteril sighed, "I'm afraid not. She was murdered in Asda's car park shortly after leaving."

Both men blanched. Paul regained his voice first. "Bloody hell!"

"Just a kid," Danny said, shaking his head. "Pretty too."

Cotteril was fuming when he arrived back at the club. He brushed passed the doorman and went straight into Dickinson's office without knocking.

Dickinson looked up sharply from a book he was reading. "Back so soon?"

"Where's the tape?" Dickinson contrived to look as if he didn't know what the sergeant was talking about. "The videotape from last night. The camera above the door."

A look of realisation came over his face, and a sickly smile. "You know? I'd forgotten all about that. Yes, the girl leaving would be on tape wouldn't it?"

"You know damn well it would be. Why didn't you offer it up when I was first here?"

"I told you. I'd forgotten. What with the shock of that poor little thing…"

Cotteril leant menacingly across the desk at him. "Don't give me any of your crap, Dickinson. You remembered well enough. Now where is it? I won't ask again."

Without removing his eyes from the sergeant's he reached into a drawer and pulled out a videocassette. Cotteril snatched it out of his hand. "Thanks." He turned and walked to the door.

"My file?" Dickinson called after him. Cotteril tossed it over his shoulder.

"You'll be hearing from us in due course," he said as he slammed out the door.

Chapter 15

In the incident room Inspector Greenwold was sitting facing the white board, which was now filling with photographs of the three crime scenes and the victims. Also on it were details of family ties, of finances and employment - with one exception, Emily. But the one thing that the inspector was studying, had not moved his gaze from in the last hour, was the photo taken from the video footage of the killer.

Cotteril burst into the room brandishing the videocassette from the Bohemia nightclub. "Sir," he ejaculated, panting from having run up two flights of stairs.

"Hmm?" Greenwold murmured not taking his eyes from the photograph.

"I've got the security video from Bohemia. They've got a camera at the front door. It's possible we'll be able to see if anyone followed Emily into the alley."

It didn't have the effect he expected. Greenwold didn't seem to hear him.

"Sir?"

"Yes, Sergeant."

"The video, sir?"

Finally Greenwold turned and looked at the sergeant. His brain seemed to catch up with his ears and he stood. "What are you waiting for? Let's go and see Warren," and he rushed out of the door with Cotteril in hot pursuit.

As he strode down the corridor, Cotteril caught up with him and asked, "What was it you were looking at, sir?"

"I'm not sure. Something but... nothing," he sighed. "There is something, not exactly wrong, but not right with the whole picture."

"How do you mean?"

"Well," he stopped abruptly, "a young girl at one-thirty in the morning hurrying home has just come out of the alley and she hears someone behind her. Someone calls her, or says something. Now wouldn't you expect her to look scared or even take flight?"

"You mean she knew whoever it was?"

"Could be. Which leads us straight back to the fact that in the case of each of the other two victims the murderer walked straight up to them and rammed a knife into them. If it were a stranger, would they have got that close or..." They continued on their way. "Oh I don't know. There's just something not right about it, that's all." He pushed the door to AV room open. "It'll come to me no doubt. I just hope it's in time."

"In time, sir?"

"Before the next one. Ah Warren, my sergeant has another video nasty for you."

In the darkened room they watched young girls and lads leaving the club in various states of sobriety until Emily came onto the screen. The three men had been passing comments up until then, but they fell silent as they watched. Warren pressed a button on the video unit, file-marking the position.

She passed Danny on the door and turned to say something to him, then laughed, bending at the waist, her eyes bright and full of joy. The other girls came into shot and each kissed Emily on the cheek and waved her away. Then they turned their attention to Danny, but the three men were straining to watch Emily as she walked out of shot.

As she left the screen Warren froze the image. "We'll need a plan of the street and the alley to figure out how far from the entrance she is," he said, scribbling furiously.

He rolled his chair to another monitor and keyboard and started frantic typing. Greenwold and Cotteril watched the screen as if by doing so they could stop her going down the alley, make her come back into shot, back to her friends where she would be safe.

The results of Warren's typing started to have an effect. The images got sharper and the contrast deepened. They could make out the pattern on Penny Abraham's slinky top. Warren rolled back alongside them. "That any better?" he asked. Neither man replied. The video started again.

Various people came and went but none of them used the alley. After ten minutes Inspector Greenwold said, "Could you rewind it to where she left the club for me, Warren?"

He moved forward on his chair and punched at some buttons on the specialist video machine and the tape wound back to the exact point Greenwold requested in a matter of seconds. "If I could transfer it onto the PC, I could get it better."

"Not just yet, I want to watch it a few more times."

The men silently watched Emily leave the club time and time again. Each time they hoped to catch a glimpse of something, anything that they could get Warren to zoom in on or whatever it is that he does, but there was nothing.

Sergeant Cotteril let out a long breath as if he had been holding it the whole time they had been there. "Sorry, sir," he said. "I hoped there'd be something for us to go on."

"Don't beat yourself up, Sergeant. It was a good try. Ok, Warren, do whatever it is you do with your computers. Let us know the instant you find something."

The two men walked dejectedly back to the incident room. There was an air of expectancy as they re-entered, they had heard about the second tape. Greenwold looked round a. shrugged. Everyone deflated as if pricked by a pin and we. back to his or her respective tasks.

Greenwold took up his station in front of the greatly enlarged picture.

"Can I get you a coffee, sir?" Cotteril asked, his eyes downcast. He just wanted something to occupy his mind. Sometimes, when you least expect it you get inspiration. Doing something as mundane as making coffee for everyone may just do it.

"That would be nice, Sergeant, thank you," he replied, almost too quiet to be heard. The sergeant wandered around the officers in the room collecting their orders and left.

It was more than a half an hour later that Greenwold realised that there was a rising murmur behind him. He tuned in to hear what was being said and it seemed to be, by a consensus, "where the hell's Cotteril with the coffee?".

The inspector leapt to his feet and charged out of the room down the corridor to Warren's den.

"What is it? What did you see?" he said as he burst through the door.

Without looking up Cotteril said, "When we watched the murder take place, the murderer went back into the alley. I thought if we watch the tape further on we may catch him coming out after the event."

Greenwold clapped him on the shoulder, "Well done." He looked at Warren. "Anything?"

"We think so, sir."

He grabbed a chair and pulled it close to the screen. "Where?"

Warren pointed to the top left corner of the screen. "Just in view, there's someone walking into and out of shot. You can only see their legs, but a few seconds later there's a dull light briefly - then it's gone."

"A car door opening we think, sir."

"No car lights? Number plate? Anything like that?"

"Sorry sir, no." Warren admitted grudgingly.

"But…"Cotteril started.

"Yes? What? But what?"

"But the two doormen, Paul and Danny, sir, they seemed quite observant when I spoke to them earlier. They may remember something if we show them this tape, sir."

"Do it!" Greenwold exploded. "Have them brought in immediately if not sooner."

Paul and Danny sat in the darkened room and studied the tape, debating under their breath what they remembered. They asked Warren to freeze on shots now and then or to run it slower over sections. Finally they looked at one another and nodded in agreement.

"Any luck?" Greenwold asked as nonchalantly as he could muster.

"Yeah," Danny said, and then looked to Paul for support. He nodded. "We're pretty sure it was a Mondeo."

"Dark blue," Paul chipped in. "03 reg."

"There was something…"

"The brake light."

"That's it. The off-side brake light didn't work." Danny smiled happily at the inspector. Then his face fell under Greenwold's expectant gaze. "No number plate, sorry."

"Only the year," Paul added.

"Thank you, you've been a great help. I mean it. Thanks to your alertness we now have a possible lead. No matter how tenuous, it's still a lead." He stood and led them to the door, shaking their hands.

"Thank you again. Sergeant could you arrange for them to the be taken home or wherever it was you dragged them in from?"

*

Greenwold burst through the doors of the incident room. "Right you lot. A dark blue Mondeo: 03 registration, offside brake light not working. Find me that car." He looked around. "Are you still here?" There was a scrabbling as officers rushed from their seats to obey his command.

A lead. They had a lead.

Chapter 16

A quick check on the Swansea computer turned up three 2003 registered dark blue Mondeos in the local area. Inspector Greenwold prayed that the killer lived locally, the number for the same car in the UK was unimaginable.

He had detectives out chasing down the owners. The first was a Mr Ramsey, a salesman for a machine tool company and on the road all day, every day, including some weekends according to his wife. This week he had been travelling in the Midlands. It would be possible to get back, do the deed, and return to his B&B in time for some sleep Inspector Greenwold calculated. Although not a likely suspect, someone who was as free as that could be a hit man and the salesman story just a cover for his trusting wife. "Like tea from China," Inspector Greenwold mused. "Far fetched."

The second owner was Mr Anderson, a pharmacist in the High Street. Poisoning would be more his modus operandi, Cotteril quipped and landed the job of checking him out as punishment.

The third was proving more problematic. The owner, according to Swansea, a Mrs Stedman, said she sold it two months ago. The buyer paid cash for it and drove it away. She didn't get his name but he was quite a large man, in his thirties with tattoos on his forearms. He was also totally bald. Mrs Stedman said that he spoke with a clear, educated accent - upper class was her description - which belied his appearance.

This upper-class heavy seemed to have vanished into thin air. Inspector Greenwold sent a handful of officers out, passing the description among their various contacts in Perry Green's criminal fraternity.

Mr Anderson was eating dinner when DS Cotteril and Constable Moore knocked on his door.

"Do come in, officers." He led them into his lounge and pulled the door to the dining room closed saying he wouldn't be long to his wife as he did so. He seated himself and bade the officers do likewise. "Now, what can I do for you?"

"Do you own a dark blue Mondeo, registration number PG03 HYY?" Cotteril asked.

He sat back, surprised. "Why, yes I do. Excuse my surprise only usually when I speak with the police it is on the matter of drugs, not my car. Have I been snapped by a speed camera?"

"No, sir. Do you know where was it parked in the early hours of this morning?"

"Where it is now, in my driveway - I hope," he added.

"And it wasn't moved from there all night?"

"No. I parked it there at six o'clock after I had locked up at the pharmacy. Then went out in it to Tesco's to do some shopping at about seven. I suppose I arrived back at eight fifteen or thereabouts and the car wasn't moved again until I went to work this morning at a quarter to eight. Why do you ask?"

"Just routine, sir. Do you have possession of both sets of keys?"

"Yes. One set are in my jacket pocket and the spare's on a hook in the kitchen. Just a moment." He got up and walked out of the room. A few moments later he returned with both sets of keys. "There you are." PC Moore took them both and compared them, then, nodding to Cotteril, handed them back.

"Is this something to do with that poor girl's death?" he asked.

"Just following up on some lines of inquiry, sir."

"I hear she was knifed, is that true?"

"I'm sure I can't say, sir," he parried. "Would you have known if your car had been taken during the night and returned before you left this morning?"

He shrugged, "I really don't know, Sergeant. I suppose it is conceivable."

"Would you mind if we get Forensics to look it over?"

"No, not at all, be my guest." Cotteril nodded to Moore who went into the hallway. The two men could hear him on his radio.

Cotteril stood to leave. "Thank you very much, sir. The team will be here shortly and they will leave your car as they've found it. Just one more thing, sir, I know we have your fingerprints on file as you are a pharmacist, but do we have your lady wife's?"

"Yes, as she helps me in the pharmacy now and then."

"Is there anyone else with access to your car?"

"No," he shook his head, pursuing his lips.

"Well thank you again, sir. Sorry you've been troubled."

"Not at all, Sergeant."

Cotteril and Moore left the Andersons to speculate about the murder. As they turned out of the road, they saw the forensics team coming the other way. "Greenwold's on their tails as well," Cotteril said. "But I don't think they'll find anything there."

"No, sir."

"Ok, back to the ranch."

Mr Ramsey was staying at an address he had told his wife was a B&B. It was not, as the officers from Coventry police found out. It was his wife's home - his other wife that is.

Mr Ramsey was obviously a very good salesman. He had sold himself to two women less than one hundred and fifty miles apart and led two very happy lives.

He was not, however, very popular with Mrs Ramsey number two that evening.

They took him into custody to face one charge of bigamy. It was also for his own safety as Mrs Ramsey number two outweighed him by a good three stone and the officers feared for his life if left there.

The bad news was, his car was in the garage at home number two and he and his wife had dined out the previous night at an Indian restaurant where they were known by the staff. He had a cast-iron alibi for the time of the murder but wished he hadn't.

Inspector Greenwold was staring at the murderer's picture when WPC Betteridge tapped him on the shoulder. "The third car has turned up, sir," she told him. "DS Mills is on the phone." She handed him the receiver.

"You've found it?"

"Yes sir," said Mills from a wasteland on the outskirts of Aylesbury.

"What on earth is it doing there?" he asked.

"Being used in a robbery sir. It was the getaway car." Greenwold groaned inwardly.

"Dare I ask when this robbery took place, Sergeant?"

"Last night, sir. At six o'clock. It was a jeweller's.

"They were just locking up for the night when three big men in ski masks forced them back into the shop and cleaned them out. The car was dumped some hours later and burned out."

Greenwold shook his head and sat down heavily in his chair. He sighed deeply. "Ok, Sergeant. Back you come, let's start again."

When Inspector Greenwold sunk back into his favourite chair that night he had a splitting headache and a longing that no

amount of whiskey could slake. Such was his inner turmoil
that he finished two large glasses before falling into an uneasy
sleep.

Chapter 17

His wife pottering around in the kitchen making breakfast wakened the inspector. He always said she made enough noise to wake the dead and this morning he was proven right. It felt like he had died many times over, he was suffering from what he called a "whiskey head" this morning. It was one of those pains that made you pull your head down into your shoulders, concertinaing your neck in the forlorn hope that it will help. He swung his legs over the edge of the recliner and thought about standing.

"You look a state," Jean said from the doorway. "Were you drinking all night?"

"Feels like it," he groaned.

"I'm doing you a fix-u-upper; it'll be ready in five minutes. Do you think you'll make it into the kitchen or shall I call the paramedics?"

"I would laugh if it didn't hurt so much."

She returned to the kitchen to supervise the making of a full English fry-up with tea thick enough to stand the spoon in. She heard him groan as he sat at the table.

"Here you go," she said, plonking it in front of him.

He looked at it, at her and at the cooker. "You not having one?"

"No. I'm eating healthy this week."

"That time of year again is it?" he asked cheekily.

"You can't be that bad if you want a fight."

The banter between them was a way of releasing the tension caused by "the job". She knew he couldn't discuss the investigation with her. It wouldn't do any good if he could, she wouldn't understand why he couldn't just arrest everyone she suggested. But she was worried, it wasn't often he got like this over a case but then again, it wasn't often they had an indiscriminate murderer on the loose.

"You want to talk about it?" she suggested gently. He thought about it while he chewed. "Shall I call Cotteril and get him to pick you up?" He nodded, still masticating on a mouthful of bacon and egg. She got up and went into the lounge where he heard her on the phone.

"He'll be here in half an hour," she said from the doorway. "I'll run the shower for you and lay out your clothes." As she passed to go upstairs he grabbed her hand and kissed it tenderly.

"Thank you," he said.

She smiled and wiped ketchup from the corner of his mouth. "Don't mention it."

When he came down, showered and changed, Cotteril was just finishing off a cup of tea. "Morning, sir."

"Good morning, Sergeant. Anything happen while I was asleep - like some knife wielding maniac give himself up?" he asked hopefully.

"Afraid not, sir."

"Oh well, I must've dreamt it then." He bent and kissed Jean on the lips. "Don't wait up."

"I never do," she smiled.

In the car silence reigned. Each man with his own, individual, thoughts sharing a single topic: "where do we go from here?"

Greenwold finally broke the silence. "Would you pay a visit to our two eagle-eyed friends at the nightclub and see if they can add anything after sleeping on it?"

"Yes, sir."

"Just drop me here, I'll walk the rest of the way." Cotteril pulled the car over and Greenwold got out. "See you at the station." He closed the door and watched him drive away.

Just around the corner was where the second murder had taken place. He stood and surveyed the two rows of garages and the heavily cambered concrete between. The chalk outline of the victim was still just visible where someone had tried to wash it away. He stood where Mr Quinn must have stood moments before the killer struck. He was looking for where his assailant had lain in wait for him. Or was it just bad timing? Would anyone have done? Was the killer killing just because he could? Perhaps it was a game? A warped and evil game, but a game all the same. He was saying, "I can kill whoever I like, whenever I like and you can't stop me." Perhaps there was no connection between the three victims, except terminal bad luck.

"Oi!" Someone shouted at him from behind. He turned but couldn't see anyone. "Oh sorry, I didn't recognise you." It was the man who had found Mr Quinn's body. "I've been watching for him."

"Sorry?"

"The killer. I've been watching for him."

Greenwold shook his head uncomprehendingly.

"They always return to the scene of the crime, don't they? Well I'll be here if he does." He hefted a baseball bat he had been concealing behind his back.

"We would rather take him alive and in one piece if it's all the same to you, sir." Greenwold said pointedly.

He just smiled. "So. Have you got anybody for it?"

He shook his head. "Our investigations are proceeding," he said automatically.

"Thought as much."

"Where did you just come from?" Greenwold had just realised what was bothering him. He hadn't seen the man until he was on top of him.

"Down there." He pointed to a row of garage doors. Green-wold still could not see where he had been hiding. "Between the third and fourth garages there's a small alleyway, just big enough to squeeze through. We all say the workmen cocked up the measurements when they built the garages and that little gap was left."

Greenwold walked to the indicated garages. There it was. A gap about two-foot wide, easily big enough for someone to be concealed.

"Which was Mr Quinn's garage?" he asked looking around.

"That one." It was two garages beyond the gap.

Greenwold reached into his pocket and dialled the station. "Greenwold here, take a look at the SOCO report for Quinn and see if Forensics covered a small alleyway or gap between garages number 112 and 114. I'll hold." He looked at the man who was waiting attentively. "I hadn't noticed that gap before... Yes," he turned his back on the man. "Get them down here immediately a Mr... He looked at the man questioningly.

"Culden."

"Culden will be waiting for them. Tell them to get the lead out, I want their report before lunch." He hung up. "Mr Culden, could I ask you to watch over this gap and not let anyone up or down until my lads have been there?"

"Sure." He nodded happily. "I'll go block the other end."

"Wait!" Greenwold just stopped him going down the alley. "That includes you. Go around and block if you don't mind, I'll wait here." Culden loped off round the corner.

Fifteen minutes later he was back, breathing heavily but smiling like a madman.

"Done it," he panted. "Put a lump of corrugated against it then lent a wheelbarrow up against that," he said, obviously pleased with his ingenuity.

"That's excellent, thank you. Now can I leave you to hold the fort until the forensics team get here?"

"Yeah sure, no problem."

"Thank you again." Greenwold strode off toward the station. "Our killer is a lurker," he said to himself.

As he entered the incident room he immediately noticed a new figure. He mainly noticed this figure because it was sitting in his chair, the chair he occupied while staring endlessly at the picture of the killer. He nodded toward the figure enquiringly; those around him just shrugged their shoulders.

"Can I help you?" he asked.

The man turned slowly round and looked at Greenwold with the creepiest, staring eyes he had ever seen. He stood slowly; it put Greenwold in mind of a blow-up doll being inflated. Finally he stood full three or four inches taller than Greenwold, who was six feet two himself, and held out a skeletal hand. "Doctor Ransom, and it's more what I can do for you, Inspector." Greenwold took the hand and was surprised by the grip; it was like steel. "I am a profiler. A poor title but a rose by any other name…" he tailed off smiling grimly.

"A profiler?"

"I get inside the head of the killer." He turned to the picture. "Give you more of an insight as to who it is you are dealing with, thereby reducing the number of suspects." He smiled again.

"You can't reduce the number of my suspects." The man raised a questioning eyebrow. "I don't have any," he said simply. "If you don't mind me asking, who assigned you to this case?"

"Your superintendent. He thought you could do with some help and was sure you wouldn't ask for yourself."

"He got that right," Greenwold muttered.

"He said you were to go and see him when you got in."

"I see." He turned to the officers in the room and clapped his hands for attention. "Ladies and gentlemen, this is Doctor Ransom. He is a profiler and now assigned to this case. You will give him as much help as he needs. He turned back to Ransom, "I assume you are to accompany me?"

"Yes." The two men left the incident room.

Superintendent Watkins was a reasonable man for a superintendent. He didn't often meddle in Greenwold's investigations, so he was curious as to why he should feel inclined to on this occasion.

"Quite simply I thought it would help. Doctor Ransom is highly respected in his line of work and usually assists the Met.

"I have been keeping a watchful eye on the investigation. Don't worry," he said as Greenwold opened his mouth. "I don't intend to interfere. I felt another pair of expert eyes may move it along, that's all. I had left word at the front desk for you to come straight to me so I could explain before you met the doctor, but, obviously, this didn't happen."

"I came in the back way," Greenwold explained. He turned to Ransom, "Have you worked on serial killings before?"

"Several. And, before you ask, no, I didn't solve all of them, only two. Which isn't bad for someone who is purely backroom staff, as it were.

"However, I did provide observations that helped in all of the cases to which I have been attached. But it's up to the likes of your good self to put my observations into context and make the arrest.

"If you would rather I wasn't here, then that's fine. I have no intention to disrupt the investigation."

Greenwold cooled down from his initial outrage and could see that everyone was just trying to help.

"I would be glad to have you on board, Doctor."

*

"Who has the forensic report from the Asda car park?" Greenwold asked when they had returned to the incident room. A hand went up at the back of the room. "Could you reassemble it and pass it to me please?" The file was passed, person-to-person to the inspector. "Is anybody covering car rental agencies and hire firms?"

"DS Wensbury, sir, he's going round them now."

"Excellent. When Sergeant Cotteril gets back I will be in the AV room with Doctor Ransom." He turned to the man. "This way, Doctor."

Warren was still running various bits of the video back and forth.

"Any luck?"

He shook his head. "I was hoping that if I changed the contrast I might get a bit more detail off the back of the car, but nothing doing."

"This is Doctor Ransom."

Warren turned in his chair, "Hiya, Doc. They pulled you in on this one then?"

"It would appear so," he replied dryly.

"You know each other?" Greenwold asked.

"Yeah, must be, oh, about five years eh, Doc?"

"Four," but he was distracted, reading through the file he had picked up in the incident room. "You do realise this is a job of work," he said.

Greenwold and Warren looked at one another. "Sorry?" said the inspector.

"Your killer. It's a job of work. Rather like, oh I don't know, someone who destroys animals. They turn up, they kill the animal, and they go home to their tea and children. A job of work."

"A professional hit?"

"Possibly, possibly. Not quite what I had in mind. More something that has to be done.

"In the video you have, the killer walks up to the young girl, stabs her, but then watch…" He pointed to the screen. "He waits until he is sure the job is done, that the girl stops moving. But he never gets near enough to contaminate the scene or become contaminated.

"Then he checks round that he hasn't been seen, a natural instinct. In the wild, a big cat having caught and killed its prey will look around to ensure there is nothing bigger that will steal its dinner. In this case it's more self-preservation.

"Then he walks off without a backwards glance. Not casually, but businesslike, as if he has an appointment elsewhere."

"Or the next victim to meet," Greenwold said ruefully.

"A job of work."

While Ransom had been speaking, Cotteril had entered the room. "You were right, sir. Paul remembered something else. There was a Hertz rental sticker in the back window. I've contacted Wensbury and he's on his way there."

"Excellent, have you met Doctor Ransom?"

"No sir, pleased to meet you," he said as they shook hands. Greenwold smiled as he noticed Cotteril wriggle his fingers afterwards, a grip like steel.

"How long before Wensbury gets there?"

"Should be there now, sir." Cotteril's phone rang at that moment. He put it to his ear, and after a second reached into his jacket pocket, pulling out a pen and his notepad. Cradling the phone on his shoulder he wrote in the pad. "We'll meet you there. Wait until we arrive. If he moves, follow but don't apprehend." He hung up.

"We've got him, sir. A dark blue Mondeo was rented out the night of the murder. It had only done seventeen miles when returned and had a blown offside brake light bulb. The man who hired it paid cash, refusing all the usual insurances they try to get you to sign up for."

"Most people do that, Sergeant."

"Yes, but according to Wensbury, sir, this man physically brushed the salesman aside and walked out."

"Not exactly professional," the Doctor observed. "Would certainly get you noticed."

"The hirer left something in the car when he returned it, some complimentary tickets for Bohemia. He was there in the club that night."

"Where is he now?" They had left the AV room and were almost trotting down the corridor toward the back door and the car park beyond.

"He's catching the one o'clock train back to London, sir."

"How do you know that?"

"His ticket fell out when he paid for the car. The salesman picked it up."

"Thank the lord for nosy salesmen eh? Let's hope he doesn't decide to catch an earlier train."

On platform four, Wensbury was casually reading a newspaper when the inspector and his entourage arrived. They insinuated themselves on the platform in ones and twos. Some getting coffee for the appearance of it, others studying the arrivals board. All surreptitiously stalking their prey. Wensbury gave an almost imperceptible nod toward a young, lean man who stood no more than five foot six tall. He wore a smart leather jacket, black jeans and trainers and carried a small valise.

The London train pulled into the station and as the man made toward the door his watchers converged on him. Green-wold cut in front at the door, turned and said, "I'm sorry," as if it were an accident. Then, as Cotteril and Wensbury grabbed him from behind, he snatched the valise from his hand.

They manhandled him to the ground, the man was screaming. "What the hell's going on? Help me! What are you doing?" Anyone who moved in his direction had a warrant card pushed in their face and a warning to back off.

Finally they dragged him to his feet, his hands cuffed behind his back. "We want words with you, chummy," Greenwold said and they frog-marched him out of the station, the guard opening the barrier, letting them pass.

Chapter 18

The suspect sat slumped in a chair behind the table in the interview room. Facing him was a two-way mirror; he was staring straight at it. He could have no idea how many people were staring back at him, but he guessed it would be at least two, possibly three. In fact, there was only one, Doctor Ransom. He was sitting very erect, close to the mirror, his hands crossed in front of him on the table. There was a notepad, a pen and a dictation tape recorder. He was ready for a long session.

After half an hour, the man shifted in his seat and shouted at the mirror, "How long you gonna be then, eh? What about a cup of tea?" He kicked the table leg viciously.

Ransom picked up his pen and made a short note on his pad, put it down and resumed his position, studying the suspect.

Having elicited no response he looked around by means of rolling his head on his neck. He stuck his bottom lip out at the mirror as if pouting; Ransom made another note on his pad.

Then he sat up, leaning his elbows on the table, staring straight at the mirror again. "So what's it gonna be, eh? You gonna starve me into submission? This your idea of softening me up, well it won't work." To emphasise the point he sat back and kicked the table again.

He had been sitting there just under an hour when Sergeant Cotteril opened the door and dragged a trolley into the room that held a TV monitor and video player.

"What's this then, *Watch with Mother*?" he said dryly. Cotteril ignored him and went back out of the room. Before he could stand to investigate the TV, Cotteril returned with a cable that he plugged between the TV and video. From his pocket he took the remote control and switched the TV to standby.

He sat with his back to the mirror. "Sorry to keep you waiting," he said. "Inspector Greenwold will be with us in a minute."

"A bloody hour I've been here. Not even been offered a cup of tea. You lot have got no manners." Cotteril ignored him. Behind the mirror the doctor made a few more additions to his list.

Five minutes later Inspector Greenwold burst into the room. He was carrying a file, a couple of evidence bags and the man's valise. "Sorry to keep you waiting," he smiled. He nodded to Cotteril who started the interview recorders and made the introductions.

"Now, let's get on with it, shall we?" Greenwold said. "This is the valise we took from you at the station. I wonder if you would open it for us please?"

"No."

"Why not?"

"Because you've planted something in there and you want me to put my prints on it, whatever it is. I wasn't born yesterday you know."

"In fact the contents of the valise are in these bags." He put the evidence bags on the table one at a time. Each was stuffed with money. "Would you care to tell us how much is there?"

"No idea. Never seen it before."

"Oh." He put on a dejected tone then, turning to Cotteril. "Well that's strange, Sergeant."

"Sir?"

"He says he's never seen it before yet his finger prints are all over them." He looked back at him. "How do you account for that?"

"You planted them there."

Both Cotteril and Greenwold burst out laughing, even he joined in after a pause.

As suddenly as he started Greenwold stopped and lunged forward. "Let's cut he crap shall we? We know who you are. We know where you're from and we know why you're here. Now, how about you start co-operating," he growled. Then he sat back, a smile wreathing his face. "Your name is George Stamp."

"Might be," George said sullenly.

"You live at number 217a, Selden Hill, Battersea, London." George shrugged as if he had never heard of the place.

"And you've just been paid off for this, Sergeant?"

Cotteril pressed buttons on the remote and the TV sprang into life, it was the footage of Emily's death.

George looked bemused at first, then curious. Then, when Emily was stabbed so viciously, he started back in shock and looked at the two policemen, his mouth open.

"That's enough, Sergeant." Cotteril switched it all off.

"What was that? What... 'Ere, you don't think... You're not..." he looked from one man to the other. "That wasn't me!" he exploded, standing up so fast his chair was knocked over. Cotteril matched his motion, taking up a posture that said "just try it chummy".

"You can't fit me up for that!" he shouted.

"Let's settle down, shall we? Sergeant, help Mr Stamp with his chair. George grabbed the chair and seated himself before Cotteril could move.

"At one thirty in morning of the 15th of May this year you stabbed and fatally wounded Emily Patterson. We would like to know why."

"But I didn't do it!" panic etching his face. "I didn't. It weren't me on that tape. It could've been anyone."

"This was taken by the security cameras outside Asda. The alley Emily and yourself emerged from leads to the Bohemia nightclub where you first saw her and where you followed her from." All the time George was professing his innocence, shaking his head. "You then walked back down the alley and got into your Hertz rental car, a blue Mondeo with a broken off-side brake light, and drove away."

"But… but…" was all he could say.

"Apart from the video, the two security men at the club remember the car."

"I wasn't me!"

Greenwold took another evidence bag and put it on the table in front of George. "This is the rental agreement you signed for the car. It's not your name, naturally, but your finger prints are on it." He put another bag on the table. "This is a pair of complimentary tickets we found in the foot well of the car, stamped the 15th May 2005, also with your fingerprints on them." Greenwold moved the first bag with all the money in it back in front of George. "Who paid you to kill her?"

George leapt to his feet again, "I didn't! Can't you hear me? I didn't kill her. You've got the wrong man. I've never hurt no one, ever." Greenwold raised his eyebrows, sat back and crossed his arms across his chest. George sank down again; he looked totally at his wit's end. Then he looked Greenwold in the eye.

"Ok, ok. Yes, I hired the bloody car. Yes I was in the bloody nightclub and yes I probably drove away at the time you said. But I was never in that alley or that car park," he said emphatically. Greenwold and Cotteril exchanged disbelieving looks.

"Look, I came here to do a bit of business, that's where the money came from, all right?"

"Five thousand pounds," Greenwold stated. "Must have been pretty serious business. And why weren't you paid by cheque? Much safer than carrying that amount of cash on you."

He shook his head. "You get paid cash in the business I'm in and you know what that is." He looked at the two men again; their faces deadpan. He sighed deeply. "Ok," he started. "It

108

was for a painting." The officers looked at one another. "I stole a painting up town. Some poncy singer from a boy band has this flat in Docklands. I crashed a party and cased the joint. Most of it was crap but there was this one painting that looked tasty. I looked it up at the library and realised it's worth quite a few bob so I went back and nicked it.

"His security system was pants. A kid could get through it. I walked in, took it and walked out again - sweet as you like. Then I spent a few days asking round and turned up a name here that'd take it off my hands. So I came up here the morning before, fenced it - the bastard fleeced me as well, it was worth ten times what that tight sod paid. I got me a B&B with the intention of getting the train back the next day.

"That night I went for a drive to find some action and maybe some company, but all I could find in this dead an' alive hole was that club. I spent a few hours in there getting knocked back by every bird I spoke to. Which ain't surprising; most of them hadn't reached puberty yet. So I had a few drinks and left. That's when the boys on the door saw me an' that's when I drove away." He looked at the two men again. "That's it. Honest. You can check if you like?"

Greenwold pushed a clean piece of paper and a pen across the table to him. "Name and address."

"What?"

"Of the face you sold it to. Name and address."

"You've got to be joking?"

"Not much of a story, wouldn't you say, Sergeant?"

"Rubbish, sir."

"Ok, ok, cut the dumb and dumber routine." He scribbled a name and address on the paper and pushed it back.

Greenwold picked it up then he and Cotteril stood, gathered up the evidence bags and left the room.

In the viewing room behind the mirror Doctor Ransom didn't wait for them to ask. "It isn't him," he said simply.

"What?" Cotteril asked incredulously.

Greenwold picked up the pad from in front of the doctor, looked at it then raised his eyebrows.

"My shopping list, sorry," the doctor said taking it back.

"Back to the incident room," Greenwold said and they followed him back out of the door.

In the incident room, Greenwold cast orders left and right, checking out what George had told them. Then settled down with the doctor. "Ok. I'm all ears."

"He is a thief, Inspector, not a murderer. His attitude has been wrong from the moment you picked him up." The doctor leant back in his chair tapping his pen against his fingertips. "He had been caught, yes, and although this is annoying for him, it isn't the end of the world, merely an occupational hazard.

"His whole attitude in the room was wrong for someone who had methodically and dispassionately killed three people. You would expect either total silence, and believe me these people can stay silent as a rock. Or they want to know how you caught them, what they did wrong.

"They can also be dismissive, superior, a 'who are you to question me?' attitude. They consider they are the top of their profession. Masters of their art, because that is what it is to them," he took a slow breath. "Or, in very few cases, they are matter of fact. 'Oh well, you caught me. Let's get on with it.' George in there is none of those things.

"I'm sorry. I know you thought you have your killer, but I don't think you have," he finished simply.

Greenwold leant toward him and said conspiratorially, "Neither do I."

Chapter 19

Greenwold stared out into the gathering night. The double-glazing muffled the sound of the traffic passing below. People were hurrying home after a long day at work or were going out to do the shopping. He knew that somewhere out there, among them, the murderer of three people was walking free, possibly stalking his next victim, and it made his blood boil.

The room behind him buzzed with the sound of his squad on the phones, at the computers, exchanging detail. In the interview room below, the fence, a distinguished member of the Roundtable who had lived among them in Perry Green for ten years, was giving a statement.

In the cells the drug dealer and his associates were being held pending their trial - that was a good bust of Cotteril's, the car was groaning under the weight of the stuff. Scott Prentice must have been the first of a long list of customers to be visited that day. The drug squad had taken over with unconcealed glee, they were sure they would get a fair portion of the supply chain from these individuals.

So, an art thief, a fence, a drug trafficker and two very hard men wanted on numerous assault charges, not to mention a bigamist - but no murderer.

He walked back and sat in front of the board again. His bum was wearing a nice groove in the chair; it was almost as comfortable as his recliner at home.

Home, yes that had been another casualty. By the time he got home these days he hardly had time to pour a whiskey before he fell asleep. His long suffering wife felt ostracised, unable to comfort her man, unable to understand the turmoil he was going through. Poor Jean, she deserved better.

He turned his back to the board and let his eyes roam the incident room. He watched Cotteril bashing away at a keyboard; he was quite a whiz on them, he noted. The police force in any area of the United Kingdom had access to exactly the same data as any other police force. It was all shared at the speed of light between the computers.

How things had come on these last ten years or so. But, the more coppers you had on computers, the less you had on the street. The victims would have been discovered a lot quicker had there been the old beat Bobbie patrolling as they used to. Would it have helped? Who knew? Maybe. Maybe not. He sighed and rubbed his eyes. This was going nowhere - the investigation had stalled.

A sound broke his reverie. He turned and looked as a coin, a penny, spun to a stop on the desk in front on him. He looked up into the hard, staring eyes of Doctor Ransom.

He smiled. "They're not worth a penny of anyone's money."

"Let me be the judge of that," the doctor said, pocketing the coin. "Would you like a sounding board? A very expensive sounding board that often answers back, I grant you."

"The jury's out on chummy downstairs but I'm pretty sure they will find that he's no more than what he says he is - a thief fencing a piece of art. Which puts us right back at square one."

"How so?"

"Sorry?"

"Why square one? You're learning every step of the way. It may not be what you want to learn, but until it is put aside, done and dusted, you can't move on."

"The car was a red herring. We burned a lot of time and resource going down any number of blind alleyways," Greenwold said, frustrated.

"But you had to unclutter yourself of it. It had to be eliminated from the investigation."

"I know," he sighed. "I know. But it hasn't got us any nearer to the killer."

The doctor looked as if he was going to say something but thought better of it as Greenwold continued.

"What I'm worried about, what I'm *really* worried about is that sometime soon someone is going to come through that door and say, 'there's been another one.'"

The doctor nodded his head solemnly. "Why don't you go home?"

"What?"

"Go home. What more can you do today? If the killer is going to strike again, will you prevent it by being here?" He was right of course, but Greenwold felt that would be giving in. It would be admitting he was beat, and he wasn't, not by a long chalk.

"Tell me, doctor," he asked. "Have you any view of this person? Anything that has struck you, no matter how obvious you think it may be?"

The doctor pulled a chair over and sat next to Greenwold, both men now viewing the board. "Run it by me again."

Greenwold sighed and recited the order of events as if in a dream. "Mr Prentice was found on the path in the park. His wife hadn't realised he hadn't come home. It transpires he had a lover, who he had set up in a flat overlooking the park. He used money embezzled from his business so that she, his wife, wouldn't be any the wiser."

"Don't you find that significant?"

Greenwold looked puzzled. "What?"

"That he was murdered in full view of the love nest he had set up?"

"Initially yes, but the other murders scotched that idea. There must be another motive, one we haven't seen yet. A link between the victims we haven't uncovered."

The doctor looked doubtful but Greenwold continued. "He has two children who are bleeding him dry, the boy is known to the police in Oxford and involved in drugs, but probably only as a user. The girl is off all over the world with her very upper-class friends, I would hate to think what that costs him. The mother dotes on the kids, particularly the girl, but is getting tired of the boy's antics."

"What does she do?"

"The mother? We haven't found out yet. She claimed she had a typical executive wife's life - coffee mornings, charity work, the gym - we were pursuing that line until the second murder came in.

"The second victim lived alone. His ex-wife lives with her female lover but he acted as if they are still married and he expected to be able to win her back. But that hadn't stopped him from forming a relationship with another woman he met, albeit purely a physical relationship on his part. There are no children here, and no skulduggery with his business.

"The third victim you know about. A young girl, out for the night with her friends. Still at school, an excellent pupil with prospects."

The doctor bit his bottom lip as his eyes stared into some alternate dimension from the one Greenwold inhabited. "Are you sure they are all the hand of the same person?"

"Yes, well, as far as we can tell. There is very little forensic evidence at any of the crime scenes. The killer, as you have seen, strikes once and at arm's length. Always leaving the murder weapon in the victim, the weapon being a common or garden kitchen knife available almost anywhere. And no, they are not the same brand of knives: all were different makes.

"The victims are always killed in a public place, lots of false trails for anyone to follow, and always on a hard, dry surface."

"And you can find no link between the victims?"

"None."

"Perhaps the killer is the link." Greenwold looked confused. "What I mean is, they are not linked in any way until the killer strikes. They are random targets."

"So we're chasing someone who gets off on killing?" said Greenwold, not letting on that the same thought had occurred to him. He wanted to hear the doctor's reasons, to see if they made sense.

The doctor nodded. "It 's a possibility."

"Ok. So what would be the killer's profile?"

"Ah," the doctor went into his trance again. "Difficult," he said eventually. "There is no indication of a sexual motive, not just targeting men. Not envious, at least not of the wealth, possessions or status of the targets." He thought again. "Power would be the key here, unless we 've missed something. Yes, power, the power to commit the ultimate crime without being traced. The power to thwart your best efforts.

"I assume," he said, a wistful look on his face, "you have not received any taunting correspondence or phone calls?" Greenwold shook his head. "Nothing on the web, you're monitoring the chat rooms?" He shook his head again.

"I think," he continued, "we are looking for someone who has been oppressed all their life. Someone who has something to prove.

"They probably have a mundane job and enjoy the secret thrill of knowing what they have done and no one around them suspects anything."

"Christ, Doc! That could be half the population," Greenwold said exasperated.

"No. It is someone who feels they have the right to behave the way they have. To exact their revenge for the shoddy way they are treated.

"They may have been told they haven't got enough dynamism and may have been side-lined for promotion or have seen younger people leap-frog them in their careers."

"This isn't helping," Greenwold interrupted.

"Isn't it?" the doctor seemed genuinely surprised. "I'm sorry, I thought it would," he contined unperturbed.

"It may be that they are known to you for something petty, shoplifting maybe. Something that, on top of everything else, would make them set out to 'show you' that they are better than that."

"So we look into all the shoplifters in town?"

"Not shoplifting exclusively. I was just using it as an example. Someone who overreacted when arrested or held."

It was Greenwold's turn to stare into space. "Thank you, Doctor," he said eventually. "That has helped."

"Only too pleased to have been of some service. Now I intend to partake a pint or two of the finest ale Perry Green has to offer. Can I tempt you to join me?" he said, standing and pulling on his coat. "I'm 'in the chair' as I believe they call it."

"No. Thanks all the same. I think I'll work over what you've come up with."

"I could help?"

"No, no, that's ok. You go off and have your pint. Try the Kings Arms in Tennyson Drive."

"Thanks for the tip, I'll see you tomorrow." But Greenwold's mind was already elsewhere so the doctor took his leave of him.

Chapter 20

Inspector Greenwold was in a deep sleep when PC Moore shook him awake.

"Sir?"

"Hmm?"

"Sorry to wake you, sir, but there's been another one."

He was instantly awake. "Where? When?"

"Not an hour ago."

"What time is it?" he said, squinting at his watch that doggedly stayed out of focus.

"One-forty sir."

"Does Cotteril know?" he said, getting up and gathering his discarded jacket and tie.

"No, sir, I'll call him now."

While PC Moore was calling Cotteril, Greenwold collected his thoughts. Damn it! Another one. Where did Moore say? "Where was it, Constable?" he called across the room as he searched for his shoes, he realised he couldn't remember taking them off.

"Tennyson Drive, sir. Outside the Kings Arms."

Greenwold's blood froze in his veins. "Do we know who the victim is?"

"Not yet, sir. The report has only just come in." He put the phone down. "DS Cotteril will meet us there, sir."

Tennyson Drive was ablaze with strobing blue lights from the assembled police vehicles. The crime scene was just twenty or thirty yards from the pub door. A young woman was draped in a blanket, leaning against a police car. The officer with her saw the inspector and made his way over.

"This young lady found the body, sir. It's Sally Davis, the barmaid of the Kings Arms, she almost fell over him."

Greenwold walked toward the body on the ground. "Do we know who it is, Constable?"

The officer looked from the inspector to PC Moore then back again. "They didn't tell you, sir?"

Greenwold stopped dead in his tracks. "Didn't tell me what?"

"It's one of ours, sir. At least, not exactly one of…"

"Spit it out, man!"

"It's that profiler, sir. Doctor Ransom."

Greenwold swayed. He had prayed it wouldn't be him. He had sent him there himself. Sent him to the Kings Arms and to his death. In a quiet voice he said, "Are you absolutely sure, Constable?"

"I'm afraid so, sir. Colin, the pathologist, positively identified him."

"Oh God," Greenwold sighed.

Colin had spotted him and was making his way hastily over. "I'm sorry, Joe. It's Ransom. Same MO, knife through the chest.

"Do you know why he was here? Was he meeting someone?"

"No. He wasn't meeting anyone. He didn't even know of the place until I told him last night." He looked at his old friend. "He asked me to come along for a drink but I stayed at the office. He asked where he could find a good pint and I…"

Colin patted Joe compassionately on the shoulder. "You weren't to know. You couldn't have known. The barmaid said he was quite chatty. Seemed to just be enjoying a drink. I just thought maybe he'd got a tip-off or something. I didn't know why he should have chosen here."

Greenwold nodded. "I'll have a talk to Sally."

She stood up straight as she watched the men walk over to her. Recognising Inspector Greenwold and Constable Moore she smiled wanly.

"Hello Sally, how are you feeling?" he asked gently.

"Pretty shaken up."

"I understand you found him?" She nodded. "Can you tell me what happened?"

"I locked up as usual after we'd got rid of the last of the hangers-on. Then I cleared up while Dave, the landlord, cashed up.

"Dave lives above the pub but I live in the High Street, above the Cyber Café, so I said goodnight and left."

"What time was this?"

"About twenty-five to one. We were later than usual because we had to put on a couple of new barrels for lunchtime. That's not unusual, we often do it," she explained. "Sometimes Dave, sometimes me. He makes it up in my wages if I stay behind. He's good like that." She realised she was rambling and stopped, biting her lip. "Sorry," she said.

"That's ok." Greenwold replied kindly. "And you left the pub?" he said, gently moving her on.

"Yes, sorry. Dave locked the door behind me and I started walking home. I didn't even see him. I caught my foot on something and nearly went over, then I saw…" she stopped as her eyes filled with tears.

"Just a couple more questions, Sally." She nodded. "Did you touch him? Try to roll him over? Anything like that?" She shook her head. "Did you see anyone else in the street? Anyone running away? Or hear footsteps?" Again she shook her head. "A car starting or driving off?"

Again she shook her head and breathed "No."

"Ok Sally. Thank you. I'll get an officer to take you home. Would you like someone to stay with you, I could get a WPC…"

"No. I'll be all right." She smiled gamely.

"Let me know if you think of anything else. Anytime, night or day. Here's my card, my home number is on the back." He turned to PC Moore. "Would you take Sally home please, and make sure she's safe inside."

"Yes, sir." He put a protective arm around her shoulders and led her to the car.

Greenwold was watching the men loading Doctor Ransom's body into the mortuary van when Cotteril came alongside him. "Sorry, sir, I was…" he stopped when he saw his superior's grim expression. "Who was it?"

"Ransom." He seemed to pull himself upright. "Right, Sergeant, I want every door down this street knocked up and everybody asked if they saw or heard anything after eleven o'clock. Anything at all.

"I want the area searched, all of the alleys and front gardens; anywhere someone could hide in wait. I'm going to talk to the landlord. It's just possible the killer followed Doc out of the pub." He stalked off to the pub door, which opened as he arrived. Dave stood aside to let the inspector through then closed the door again.

He went round behind the bar. "You look like you could do with a stiff one," he said, picking up a glass.

"Yes I could, and that's exactly why I won't have one. But don't let me stop you."

Dave pursed his lips and nodded, then poured himself a double whisky.

"I remember your friend last night. He was what I call a good customer. He liked a drink, was no trouble, chatted amiably with Sally and myself as well as some of the customers."

"Anyone in particular?"

He thought a moment. "Not that I can recall.

"We had a good crowd in and that kept me and Sally busy until closing. He was one of the last to leave."

"What time?"

Dave looked sheepish. "Midnight."

"Did you notice if anyone followed him out or maybe left very shortly before him?"

Dave clicked his tongue and drew breath across his teeth. "Hard to tell. As I said, he was one of the last to leave so there were about four or five going at the same time."

"Did you happen to notice which way they went from here?"

"Sorry. But I do know who they were." He squinted at the ceiling. "There was George and Tom, always here to the last. Young Eddie Black. Mike from the betting office and your friend."

"Do you have addresses for any of these?"

"George and Tom live just down the road. I don't know the numbers but I can point them out. Eddie lives in the high-rise and Mike above the bookies."

"Apart from the deceased, were there any other new faces among the crowd?"

"Not that... Hang on though. Yes there was. And he spoke to your man." A look of concentration spread across his face. "He was about young Eddie's height, five-eight, five-nine. Thin, with slicked back hair that looked black but he had so much grease on it, it could've been brown. He had a car outside, I remember him talking about it. A Ford I think." He suddenly stopped and looked excited. "He talked to Sally a lot, trying to chat her up. She'll remember him, she has a mind like a steel trap that girl."

"When did he leave?"

"Oh, about half-eleven. Made a point of telling everyone he had a meeting or something early next day. Trying to look important sort of thing. We get 'em in here." He forced a laugh.

"Do you remember anyone else leaving at the same time?"

"Yes. Now you mention it. Someone held the door for him then followed him out." He looked down at the bar top, tapping his fingers. "Who was it now," he said to himself.

"Eric!" he almost shouted. "Eric Bishop from the café. He said goodnight to Sally while he held the door open. She rents the room above his café you know. Of course you know, listen to me," he added.

"Is there anything else you can remember as being odd?"

Dave gave him an old fashioned look. "In here? Odd is normal for this place."

"You know what I mean."

"No, sorry, I wish I could." He held his hands out, palms up apologetically.

"Thanks Dave. Here's my card. If you think of anything else, call me."

"Will do," he said, looking at the card then pocketing it.

"We may be back tomorrow to ask you more questions."

"I'll be here, don't worry. And Joe?" Greenwold stopped as he reached the door. "I'm real sorry about your friend."

"Thanks."

Outside, Greenwold paused on the step and took in the activity around him. There were irate citizens on their doorstep, waving their arms at the hapless policemen charged with questioning them. The area around where Ransom fell appeared to have a beast with four pair of legs crawling over it as the white suited and booted officers searched every crevice in the pavement – and there were a lot as this was one of the oldest, original roads in Perry Green and the council had never re-paved it. Others could be seen climbing over fences and searching alongside houses, torches in hand. It was a surreal sight that met his eyes.

Cotteril ran over to him. "Nothing yet, sir."

"Right, come with me. I want to talk to Eric Bishop and Sally Davis again and I haven't got my car."

Sally was still up as the inspector expected. She was wrapped in a huge, fluffy robe with Garfield slippers on her feet cradling a mug of something steaming in her hands.

"Sorry to bother you again so soon, Sally."

"That's ok," she said, leading the way. Both men noticed her tear-stained face and red eyes. She sat on a big armchair, curling her feet under her. Greenwold and Cotteril sat facing her.

"I was talking to Dave and he said there was someone in tonight he hadn't seen before. About five-eight, five-nine with slicked back hair. He said this man was trying to chat you up?"

She stared into space a while. He thought maybe she hadn't heard him. As he opened his mouth to repeat the question she suddenly woke from her reflective state.

"Yes. I remember him. He was talking to your man as well.

"He said his name was Arthur. He's a salesman for some big computer company, was going on to your friend about his car."

"Did you catch what car it was?"

"Oh yes. Anyone for at least ten yards was in no doubt he had a Toyota Celica outside. Last year's model I think he said. I think he was full of shit though." She blushed. "Sorry." Greenwold smiled and nodded encouragingly. "Well, your friend started asking him about it and he didn't seem to know much. But he waved the keys in the air to prove it." While she had been talking, Cotteril had stood and made his way to the door. He was calling in the car description as she spoke.

"Do you know what colour?"

"Red. What else? A poor man's Ferrari. Penis extension." She put her hand over her mouth. "Sorry, I don't know what's got into me tonight. I wouldn't usually talk like this to a policeman."

"That's ok. You're doing fine." Cotteril returned and sat down again. "You've been very helpful. We only have a brief description of the man, could you help?"

"Yes. He had brown hair, dark, slicked back as you said. Leather jacket; very close fitting. The way it moved it looked expensive. Jeans. A bit tatty at the trouser cuffs and pockets. But not trendy tatty, just very worn. Brown boots. I remember them distinctly. They were obviously his second pride and joy as he kept buffing them when he was sitting. Oh and he had an earring in his left ear, just a gold hoop. Oh, and his teeth were… yuk! Dingy, stained. As if he hadn't cleaned them in years." She thought a bit longer. "That's it. Sorry I can't…"

Greenwold held his hand up, "I wish all witnesses were as observant as you. That's perfect.

"Just one last thing. Do you know where Eric Bishop lives?"

"Yes. Number 18, Keats Way, why?"

"Apparently he left at the same time as this man. We wondered if he saw which way he went. Well, thank you again for your help, sorry to keep you up."

"I don't think I can sleep anyway," she said, standing to see them out.

"Goodnight. Be sure to lock the door behind us, won't you."

"Don't worry, I will."

It took a full fifteen minutes to get a response to their knocking at Eric Bishop's door. Eventually the man opened it wearing just a pair of stained boxer shorts and a puzzled expression. "What do you want? Do you know what time it is?"

"May we come in, sir?" Greenwold asked, flashing his card and pushing past him.

"Do I have a choice?" he answered, closing the door behind them.

Greenwold stood in Eric's living room. "We need to ask you some questions about your movements tonight."

"Why?"

"There was an incident outside the Kings Arms, a man was killed and we understand you were there?"

"Yes. I was there. But I didn't see anything. That's awful," he said, sitting down in a ratty looking armchair.

"Could you tell me what time you left the pub?"

"Eleven thirty."

"You seem very sure?"

"I am. I looked at my watch and figured I wouldn't get another drink so I went home."

"Did you talk to anyone as you left?"

"Yes. There was some irritating little prat going on about his bloody car. He button-holed me on the way out."

"Did you see him drive off, sir?"

"Yes."

"Which way did he go?"

"Back to the High Street. He's staying at the hotel."

"You say 'back' to the High Street?"

Eric grinned, "I got a lift home off him. Serves him right for boring me about his bloody car."

"Did he tell you his name at all?"

"Arthur something or other, Arthur Pritchard, that's it. And he's at the Red Lion hotel in the High Street. Why, what's he done?"

"We don't know that he's done anything yet," Greenwold said, moving toward the door. "Thank you for your help, Mr

Bishop. We may call back if we need to ask you any more questions. Goodnight."

"Good morning you mean," he said sarcastically to the closing door.

Chapter 21

Two armed policemen joined Greenwold and Cotteril at the Red Lion hotel. The receptionist told them that Mr Pritchard was occupying room 213 on the second floor and was not alone as she handed over the passkey.

As quietly as they could, using both the lift and the stairs, they met in the corridor outside of room 213. Inspector Greenwold, standing to one side of the door, knocked and called out "Room service." There was a muffled discussion from the other side of the door that got louder as a male voice was asking who gave the other occupant permission to order bloody room service.

A man answered the door and was immediately lifted bodily and carried to the far side of the room where he was slammed up against the wall. His female companion screamed until Cotteril flashed his warrant card at her. She glared at the men.

Once things had settled down and the room searched for weapons, Mr Pritchard was dumped unceremoniously on his rear end in a chair and told to shut up complaining. Gemma, his companion, wanted her say.

"What the bloody hell do you think you're doing coming in here like the bleedin' SAS?"

"Sorry, Gemma, did we spoil a special moment?" Cotteril asked sarcastically.

Gemma was well known to most of Perry Green constabulary as a "working girl", as they euphemistically put it.

"Huh! Not with that one. All talk. I suppose you're going to tell me he's not into computers or loaded with money?"

"We are taking Mr Pritchard, or whatever his name is, in for questioning. Aren't we?" he asked the man who was being frog-marched out of the door, his hands cuffed behind him.

"What are you doing? You've got the wrong man. I haven't done anything. Get your hands off me, oof!"

"Sorry, was that the wall we bumped you up against?" one of the constables manhandling him through door said without a trace of sorrow in his voice.

"You'll have to come along too, Gemma," Inspector Greenwold said. She snorted and started collecting her clothes together.

"What's he done? Why am I being pulled in?"

"He is wanted to help with our inquiries and you... Well I suppose you'll be helping too." She looked as if she didn't believe him but got dressed and followed the men to the lift.

By the time they got to the interview room Arthur Pritchard was protesting vehemently about his mistreatment and the invasion of his privacy.

"I want my lawyer. You can't treat decent people like this. It isn't a police state you know."

"That is your prerogative. However, we would just like to ask you some questions." He suddenly went quiet and looked shifty. "I believe you were at the Kings Arms last night. What time did you leave?"

"Eh? Oh, about half eleven. I gave some bloke a lift home, he can vouch for me."

"What was this person's name?"

"Oh, err, Eric something or other, I didn't catch his last name."

"And what did you do after dropping him home?"

128

"I came back here. Went into the bar, but it was shut, then went up to my room."

"And at what time was this?"

"Buggered if I know. About twelve I would guess."

"And then what did you do?"

"Well, I called for room service, if you know what I mean."

"And at what time did your 'room service' arrive?"

"One. She was busy when I called. It was just before one when she arrived."

"And she was with you until we arrived?"

"Yes, until you barged through my door. Bashing me against the wall. What's it all about anyway? Why are you asking me all this stuff?"

Greenwold ignored him. "At what time did you leave the person you gave a lift to?"

"Um, probably quarter to twelve. It was only a couple of streets away." He watched Greenwold noting the times down.

"And you went up to your room at about twelve."

"Probably a little after, but no later than ten past, why?"

"What did you do between then and your 'room service' arriving?"

"Watched a bit of telly. Thought there might be a movie channel to get me in the mood, but there weren't."

"What did you watch?"

"Eh?"

"I said what did you watch?"

"Oh. Um. I can't remember. Um." He looked at the ceiling for the answer but it wasn't there. "Sorry, can't remember."

"Was it sport, or a film?"

He thought a moment. "Dunno. It's completely gone."

"So there was forty-five minutes between you getting to your room and Gemma arriving?"

"Something like that, yeah."

"And you can't remember what you watched all that time?"

"Well, I was getting ready for… you know. I was wandering around, not really watching it as such. It was just background noise."

"Is there anything else you can add?"

"No. Why? What's happened? Why have you dragged me here?"

"At between twelve and one o'clock a man was murdered outside of the Kings Arms. A man you had been seen talking to shortly before you left."

Greenwold stood and walked out of the door, letting the man - he was sure Arthur Pritchard was not his name - stew on it a while.

In the next room Gemma had already finished her statement.

"It's awful isn't it?" she said aghast. "That poor man."

"Yes, terrible." Greenwold picked up Cotteril's notes and sat down studying them.

"You say you arrived after one o'clock. Could you be a bit more precise?"

"No, sorry. My watch has stopped again. Bloody thing is always stopping." She held it out for his inspection, the hands at eleven-twenty. "But it was after one, definitely," she said determinedly.

"How do you know that?"

"I saw the clock in the taxi on the way to the hotel. It probably only took another five minutes after that, then another ten to get up to his room. That snooty cow on reception wouldn't let me through."

"So at around one-fifteen you reached Mr Pritchard's room?"

"Yes."

"Could you please put that in your statement?" He handed the paper back to her.

While she was writing he asked, "What did you think of Mr Pritchard?"

She laughed.

"What's funny?"

"Well, I doubt that's his name."

"Why do you say that?"

"Dunno. Just didn't seem easy with it, you know? A couple of times I said 'Arthur' and he looked puzzled. Just for a moment but, well a lot of men use a different name in my line of work." She thought a moment. "Ere, are you going to arrest me?"

"What for?"

"You know."

"I'm sure I don't know what you are alluding to, Miss Driscoll," he said, looking her straight in the eye.

"Thanks. Can I go now?"

He picked up the statement and read through it. "Yes, that will be all. We may need to call on you later though. Don't leave town will you."

"Fat chance," she said sneering.

After she had left, the inspector and Sergeant Cotteril pored over the statement and Greenwold's notes.

"Ok, so Gemma thinks Pritchard isn't his name," he said thoughtfully.

"And the time is right," Cotteril added. "He could've easily got from the Red Lion to the Kings Arms and back again."

"I think we need to question the receptionist and have a look around his room," Greenwold said standing up.

Agnetha, the receptionist at the Red Lion hotel, was on her break when they arrived.

"Sorry to take up your time like this," Greenwold said. "But it's very important that we talk with you about Mr Pritchard."

She laughed a hollow laugh.

"Is there something wrong?"

"Mr Pritchard. He can't spell his own name," she said. "He leave the 't' out, even I know there's a 't' in Pritchard and I'm from Finland."

"There might not be," said Cotteril.

"According to his credit card there is."

"At what time did he arrive back tonight?"

She pouted as she thought, "Ten to twelve. I looked at clock when he came through the door."

"Did he go out again before Miss Driscoll arrived?"

"Is that her name? I know what she is," she said meaningfully. "No I don't think so."

"Could he have gone out and come back again without you seeing him?"

Again she pouted. "Possibly. I was not at reception all the time. I make coffee to keep me awake. The kitchen is down the corridor."

"Did you see or hear from him between his going to his room and Miss Driscoll arriving?"

"He called down. Complaining about TV channels. No porno."

"What time was that?"

"Five, maybe ten past twelve. Not long after he arrived."

"Do you mind if we have a look in his room?" She shrugged and handed them the key.

His room was a mess, but they had caused most of that. There was a laptop case on the chair and a leather jacket thrown over the back of it. Cotteril went through the pockets. There was nothing else anywhere in the room. No case or holdall. No other clothes.

"Nothing there," Cotteril said, then he looked in the collar. "The price tag is still in it. Well, part of it."

"Looks brand new," Greenwold said. He picked up the laptop case and put it on the bed. Opening it, there was a laptop as expected, some pens in the pockets in the lid and some credit cards thrown in it. All bore the name Pritchard, Arthur Pritchard. Greenwold studied the signature. Cotteril had switched the Laptop on but it was asking for a password. "Bring it with you," Greenwold said and they left the room.

Arthur Pritchard, as he maintains, was looking very worried by the time they got back to him. "Look I want to make a statement," he said.

"Really?"

"Yes. It wasn't me, you know? I was in my room at the time."

"Watching TV you said." He nodded. "But you can't remember what you were watching."

"I told you. I was getting ready for her. The tart."

"Who are you?"

"Eh?"

"What is your real name?"

He did a good job of looking affronted. "Arthur Pritchard, I told you."

"Really?"

Cotteril placed the laptop on the table in front of him and switched it on. "Perhaps you would put the password in for us, Mr Pritchard?" he said.

Pritchard looked at the laptop and sighed. "Bollocks."

"Curious password don't you think, Sergeant?" Greenwold said sarcastically.

"Ok. You got me. But I didn't kill no one." He slumped back in his chair. "My name is Andrew, Andrew Deacon. I boosted the Toyota and that was on the floor under the seat. He'd left his credit cards in it so I had a little spend up."

"The leather coat?"

"Yeah an' some other stuff." He looked at them. "I didn't do no killing though."

"You have no alibi for the time of the murder. You were driving a stolen car, under an assumed name using stolen credit cards. You really expect us to take your word for it?"

"But I didn't. Look, a bit of thieving, yes fair enough, guilty. But murder? Not me. Look, check with the police in Cambridge, I'm known over there. Too bloody well known, if you catch my drift. That's why I came here. It was getting too hot."

At a nod from his superior Cotteril stood and left the room. A constable replaced him at the door.

"How much?"

"Eh?"

"How much did the car cost you?"

"I told you, I nicked it."

"Or bought it under an assumed name with the money you've been earning over here killing people."

"What are you talking about? What people? I nicked it, I told you. I ain't no killer."

"Why the girl? Prentice I can understand; he's bound to have pissed someone off. Quinn I'm not sure about but why the girl? She was only eighteen, couldn't have done any harm to anyone."

"What are you talking about? What girl? Who's this Prentice and Quinn?"

"And then you had to kill one of us." Deacon's face blanched. "Yes. You knew. You knew he was a copper. You were frightened he was getting near. Perhaps you saw him in the pub last night and thought he was on to you. So you took someone you've never seen before home, then went to your hotel and made a fuss, creating your alibi. You slipped out of the hotel in time for chucking out and killed him. Got back to the hotel where Gemma comes along to give you the rest of your alibi.

"Trouble is, you can't remember what was on TV and the receptionist can't be sure you didn't leave and come back again before Gemma arrived.

"You could've done it. You had time. It was only a ten-minute walk to the Kings Arms. Easy." Greenwold sat back. "How much? How much was he worth? A copper? Must've been a good pay packet for a copper."

He sat and watched the man closely, he looked as if someone had sucked all the air out of his lungs. His mouth hung open, his face white as a sheet. He didn't move for what seemed like minutes while it all sank in. "But," he said, and then straightened up. "I want a brief. Now. Before I say anything else, I want a brief. I ain't being fitted up for no murder."

"Murders," Greenwold emphasised the plural. "Four to be precise." Then he stood and left the room.

Chapter 22

In the incident room Cotteril was busy on the phone so Green-wold called DS Mills over.

"See if you can find out chummy's movements at the times of the other murders. I want to be sure he hasn't got an alibi like attending a police function, got it?"

He put a piece of paper in front of the inspector. "The car, sir, it was reported stolen by a Mr Pritchard two nights ago, but not here. It was taken in St Ives, the one in Cambridgeshire."

"Yes?"

"On the night of the girl's murder."

"What time?"

"We don't know. It was parked up for the day and only reported stolen when Mr Pritchard left to go home from work. He was working late and so didn't know it had been stolen until just before eight o'clock."

"But it could have been taken earlier?"

"Yes sir. It could have been stolen any time between nine-thirty when he parked it, and eight in the evening. It's only a couple of hours from there to here, three at the outside. I've got the Cambridgeshire police checking to see if they can tie down the time any tighter."

"Good man, let me know as soon as you get something."

"Yes sir."

"How about the time he booked into the Red Lion? What day and time was that?

"If we can show he was here in good time for Emily… Ah but what about Quinn and Prentice? If he only nicked the car the day before Emily's murder, where was he on those two nights?" He tapped the desk thoughtfully. "Get on to it will you? See if you can trace his movements for the days of all the murders."

"Yes sir." He returned to his chair and picked up the phone almost before he sat down.

There's a real sense of urgency now, Greenwold thought. There was before, but somehow it has increased ten-fold. I can feel it in the air, he breathed deeply. Good.

Cotteril had just put down the phone. "Sir? Seems our Mr Deacon is not only known in Cambridge but quite a few other counties as well." He referred to his notes. "He's been picked up in Leicester and Norfolk, for theft and passing stolen goods, nothing more serious."

Greenwold was deep in thought. Supposing, he said to himself, just supposing it isn't him. Is that possible? Let's turn this upside down, try to prove him innocent.

"It's the time between getting to the hotel and Gemma turning up. The gap in his alibi."

"Yes, but we know our killer is very careful. He doesn't leave forensic evidence." Greenwold sat up. "Could there be in the clothes we found him in? Have we tested his clothes?"

"I'll get on to it, sir," he picked up the phone again.

"Assuming there's nothing on him, where do we go from…" He suddenly launched himself out of his chair and strode out the door.

Perry Green had been blighted with an outbreak of CCTV cameras. They were installed by the major stores and businesses, like those at Asda, but there were also units installed by the police themselves. These covered major roads in the area and one or two municipal car parks. Plus there were a handful of speed cameras. He seriously doubted the killer would speed away from the scene, too conspicuous. But there was just the chance that one of these cameras picked up the killer, or Mr Deacon, heading up the High Street toward Tennyson Drive and the pub.

The control room for these cameras was in the basement of the police station, the only space they had available when they were installed. Constables took turns to man the screens and keep the tapes refreshed.

PC Ardington was on duty this morning; he clumsily moved his feet off the desk at the inspector's entrance and straightened his shirt and tie.

"Glad to see you take it so seriously, Constable."

"Sorry, sir."

"Where are the tapes for last night, top end of the High Street nearest Tennyson Drive?"

He reached to a rack in front of him. He had been in the process of updating the logbook and was able to pick them out immediately. "What time sir?"

"Chucking out time and an hour after."

He mounted a cassette in the player and fast-forwarded to the twenty-three hundred hours time stamp. The two men watched the tape in silence, Greenwold keeping a wary eye on the time code in the bottom right-hand corner.

A few cars came and went and some late night revellers heading for Bohemia or the chip shop, but no Mr Deacon and no suspicious person in leatherette.

Greenwold looked at the map pinned to the wall with the CCTV and speed cameras marked on it. There were none in Tennyson Drive itself - something he intended to rectify if they ever got to the bottom of this. "You'd think they'd have them outside of every pub, wouldn't you?" he asked, mostly of himself.

"Ok, Constable. If you were a despicable murderer who has targeted the Kings Arms public house to find a victim, which route would you use to get there?"

"On foot or by car, sir?"

"Both."

They scrutinised the map, the constable jotted some notes on a pad in front of him. Then he reached for the log and selected the corresponding tapes from the rack.

"Firstly by car sir. There are three roads covered by cameras that lead to Tennyson Drive. Are we looking for the same time stamp?" Greenwold nodded. The constable slotted the first tape into the machine. "This one is the top end of Keats Road, the far end from Tennyson." He slotted another into the adjacent player, "And this is at the junction of Tennyson and the West Road, sir. With the one in the High Street, you have them all."

"Ok, Constable, we'll watch the High Street for cars or people and then find them at the relevant times on the other two to be sure they've passed through the area. Any that don't come out the other end must be either residents or have another way out not covered by the cameras. Then we do the same for the other two cameras, ok?"

"Yes sir." He punched up the High Street tape and ran forward to pick up the first car, a Vauxhall Corsa. Then he ran the other two tapes to the same time stamp and watched them until the Corsa reappeared.

They were on the third person walking their dog when Cotteril came in the room. "Wondered where you'd gone, sir."

"Hmm?"

"I've got some info on Deacon. It couldn't have been him."

Greenwold's head snapped round to face the sergeant. "How so?"

He was in Cambridge on the night of Prentice's murder, positively identified by a sergeant there in the middle of an argument in a pub. Apparently he was trying to sell something to the original owner and a fight broke out. No charges were brought because the owner suddenly remembered he had given the item to Deacon a short while before. Blamed the beer, sir, says it made him forget. But it was definitely Deacon, sir, no doubt about that."

Greenwold thumped the desk irritably. "And the nights Quinn and Emily were slain?"

"Nothing for those, sir, only the night of Prentice."

Greenwold turned to the constable. "Keep on this; I want to know everyone who disappears into the area not to be seen again. I'll send Warren down to help; he knows what we're looking for.

"Come on, Sergeant, let's have another cosy chat with Deacon."

"He's got a brief with him, sir."

Greenwold stopped in his tracks. "Has he indeed? That was quick wasn't it? Well let's not keep the man waiting, it'll be costing him a fortune," he smiled ruefully.

"I demand that you release Mr Deacon immediately, and you may be brought up on charges of wrongful arrest or the unlawful detention of my client." His face was the rosy red of a true imbiber. James Conner of Conner, Conner and Son - the senior Conner that is - stood and wagged a tobacco stained finger at the inspector as he entered the room.

"Hello, James. I was just saying to the sergeant, you were very quick off the mark tonight, wasn't I, Sergeant?"

"Yes, sir." They sat opposite Deacon and Conner.

"Mr Deacon has prepared a statement out of civic duty to help you eliminate him from your inquiries." He handed three pieces of paper over to the inspector.

"And what inquiries are these you are referring to?" he said, reading through the papers, half ignoring the men in front of him.

140

"The murder inquiries of course. My client was nowhere near the scene of the crime as well you know."

"Do I?" the inspector raised an eyebrow. "And how would I know that?"

"If you read the statement…"

Greenwold held up a hand silencing him. Finally he put the pages down. "That all seems to be in order," he said folding his hands over the papers. This seemed to confuse Conner, and then he stood and started to fasten his briefcase. "There is however," the inspector smiled at them, "the question of the stolen car, laptop and credit cards. Also the fraudulent use of said cards to purchase a leather jacket and, if I'm not mistaken, a pair of boots and a night of ecstasy with Gemma Driscoll." The lawyer sat down again and opened his case. "You didn't really think we would forget, did you?"

"I thought as Mr Deacon was assisting you in the much larger task of your hunt for a murderer…" he tailed off.

"Yes?" Greenwold prompted.

"Well," was all Conner had to say on the subject.

"You thought we'd say 'that's ok, keep the car, jacket, boots, cards and laptop as a reward for helping us'." He smiled again. That smile was really beginning to irritate Conner.

"I thought there might be some give and take, yes."

"Well nobody gave to Mr Deacon, but he took all the same, didn't he?

"We will of course be pressing charges and Mr Deacon will be held in custody pending his hearing."

"I think bail is the least…"

"Not a chance. You see, we've been talking to the police forces in Cambridge, Leicester and Norfolk and I think they may want to talk to Mr Deacon too. So if it's all the same to you I think we will hold him here for the time being.

"Constable, find Mr Deacon a comfy cell would you. Is that all, Mr Conner?"

Conner stood huffily and repacked his case and stomped out of the room.

"Bloody load of good he was," Deacon said angrily as he was led away.

There were only two cars and five on foot - all dog walkers - who were unaccounted for on the tapes. Warren made the best job he could of improving the stills taken from the video so they could be eliminated, but it would be a painstaking task to track them all down. Officers were duly dispatched and Greenwold returned to his seat in front of the board in the incident room.

The board now had photographs of Doctor Ransom and the area around where he fell posted. Greenwold sighed deeply when he saw them. If only... If only he had hadn't told him the Kings Arms. If only he had said, "Yes, ok, I'll come for a drink with you." If only. He knew this would haunt him.

He turned to the desk groaning under the weight of reports and statements from all four crimes. He sighed again; they would all have to be gone through again, and again until something stuck, or until the questions had all been answered.

Had the victims been selected? If so, why? What drew the killer to them? Were they just in the wrong place at the wrong time? Had the killer found somewhere as an ideal place to do the deed, then simply waited until the opportunity had arisen?

But the real question, the one that had been gnawing at his soul was why? Why was the killer killing?

Chapter 23

This was the worst time of the day for Inspector Greenwold. The gathering of the night; street lamps flickered on, cars switched from side lights to main beam, shop fronts were shuttered and the good citizens of Perry Green were home having their tea - or dinner depending on which side of town you lived.

This was when he looked back over the day to analyse how much farther he had got in the inquiry, how much closer to the truth. The answer was... none. Yet another thief had fallen foul of the murderer, for that is how it seemed to him. Each time they thought... No, scratch that. Each time *he* thought he was closer to the truth, he ended up uncovering some other menial crime. Another felon was enjoying the hospitality of Perry Green nick and the murderer was snug and warm somewhere, possibly waiting for his tea - or dinner.

The day had been spent going over all the statements, not a job he enjoyed, and picking over the crimes they had uncovered. He was no nearer to knowing who the killer was, or why he killed, but at least the desk looked tidier.

The board also looked entirely different now. He had ripped all the photos and notes off it in a fit of pique and reassembled it more to his liking. There were four new columns, each with a photo of the victim at the top - Prentice, Quinn, Patterson and Ransom - beneath that, the photo of the crime scene. Each column then had notes about the victim's address, marital status, dependants, financial situation, extra-marital significant others and known associates.

Above everything - dead centre - was the still taken from the video of the killer. Warren's wizardry had not been able to improve it much; it was too far away and too deep in shadows. Alongside this picture was all that Greenwold could remember of Ransom's profile of the killer.

"Right," he said, startling Cotteril who was nearly asleep. "We have to take it from the top."

"Sir?"

"We are missing something; I know we are. Something…" he waved vaguely at the board. "There." He ended and let his arm fall to his side. "From the top. Tomorrow, we talk to the Prentice family again, and the love interest of Mr Prentice again. Then we talk to Quinn's ex, her partner, his love interest and his employer." He stopped suddenly. "Tell me we spoke to his employer," he said, a worried look on his face.

"DS Mills spoke to his employer, sir." He handed Green-wold a sheet of paper recording the salient facts of the interview. Greenwold breathed a sigh of relief.

"Then we speak to Miss Patterson's friends and family again, her schoolteachers and neighbours.

"Then…" His shoulders drooped. "Then we find out what cases Ransom had been working on lately. He said that possibly the only thing connecting the victims is the fact that they were all killed by the same person: nothing more than that. The killer is showing us he can kill at will, and we can do nothing about it."

"God!" Cotteril said aghast. "Let's hope he got that wrong. With no forensic and no leads all we can do is wait…"

"Quite."

"But you don't agree?" Cotteril said, more in hope than making an observation. "With Ransom I mean."

"No. I can't subscribe to his theory. Which means…" He turned to the board again. "We're missing something. Tomorrow, meet me at the Prentices', first thing."

"Yes, sir, goodnight, sir."

"Goodnight, Sergeant."

In his reclining chair he placed the empty whiskey glass on the table at his side. Jean came into the room, a worried expression on her face. Joe wasn't sleeping well. He never got a good night's sleep when he was on a murder inquiry, but this one was biting deeper than any she had seen before.

"Like to talk about it?" she offered.

He sighed. "That's all I can do, talk about it."

"Oh, I'm sure something will break. It always does," she tried to reassure him. She sat on his lap, her arms about his neck. "You're trying too hard. You know that when you let something go, you get inspiration." He nodded, more to make her feel better than to agree. He must be a pain to live with when he was like this.

"Where shall we go on holiday," he asked, forcing a smile to his lips and his thoughts at a tangent.

"Let's not go abroad," she said. "I'm fed up with all the messing about in the airports and with the taxis at the other end. Let's stay in England." She looked into his eyes, "Or Scotland or Wales. Hey, how about Ireland? We've never been there. I've heard it's lovely and the people are the nicest you could ever wish to meet."

Jean, he reflected, was not one of nature's globetrotters. No matter how excited she got about going to some far-flung foreign land, once she got to the airport she was a bag of nerves. She could plan it meticulously for months in advance, but once through the doors into the airport, she would happily turn on her heel and go straight back home.

"That's sounds lovely," he said. "You're right, there's so much to see right on our doorstep, and they even drive on a civilised side of the road." Joe hated driving on the right. He was a danger to all traffic, and some pedestrians, when he had to negotiate not only the wrong side of the road, but also the gear lever and handbrake emigrating to the right.

"What about those Center Parcs?" Jean said excitedly. "Audrey, my hairdresser, swears by them. And they're all set in lovely forests, trees everywhere," she laughed, "so many you can't see the wood."

It was then. That moment. Those few words. Greenwold felt as if someone had tipped a pint of ice water over his brain. He realised he had been walking around in a fog, but now - now it was crystal clear.

Jean felt the change in his bearing. "What?" she asked. "What have I said?" He smiled and kissed her passionately, so much so that Jean felt as if all the air had been taken from her.

"You are wonderful," he said simply. "I am so fortunate to have married you."

"Oh Joe," she said coyly and blushed. He kissed her again. "You've done it haven't you? You've had a brainwave."

He grinned, put his thumb against his temple and waggled his fingers. "Yep."

"And now you're going to go out and get back to work again. Ok, I'll see…"

"Nope," he said, picking her up bodily. "We," he continued as he carried her from the living room, "are going to bed."

The following morning Joe was whistling as he dressed. Jean lay back in the bed, a contented expression on her face. "Who was that on the phone?" she asked, not really caring what the answer would be.

He poked his head round the door of the en suite bathroom. "Me." He smiled that irritating smile he had when he was being playful, and ducked back out of view.

"You know what I mean, who were you talking to? Not poor Cotteril? Not at this time in the morning?"

146

He strode back into the room adjusting his cuffs. "Twenty-four, seven - as our colonial friends like to say. That's what this job is; twenty-four/seven."

"So what did I say?"

"Hmm?" He pretended not to know what she meant.

She got out of bed naked, and grabbed him around the neck, having to stand on tiptoe to reach. "If you don't tell me," she warned, "I'm going to pull you back into bed and ravage you until you beg for mercy."

He laughed happily and kissed her upturned face. "The trees."

"Eh?"

"The trees. You can't see the wood for the trees." He was enjoying teasing her.

"And?"

"So where would be the best place to hide a tree?"

She looked at him a long moment, then let go and climbed back into bed. "If you're going to talk gibberish, Joe Greenwold, you can go to work un-ravished," she pouted.

"Where would be the best place to hide a tree, Sergeant?" Greenwold asked as they walked down the corridor to the incident room where, he hoped, the rest of the squad were assembled, summoned by Cotteril's earlier phone calls.

"Sir?"

"Humour me."

"I don't know." He thought a while as they walked. It's way too early for conundrums. "I don't know, sir."

"In a forest, Sergeant." He looked at Cotteril meaningfully.

"We have four bodies, but only one was a candidate for murder. We find which one and we find the murderer." He marched into the incident room leaving Cotteril with a puzzled expression on his face. He shrugged and followed his superior.

Greenwold called them all to order in his customary fashion. "Ladies and gentlemen," he called out over the hubbub. When he was sure he had everyone's attention he continued. "The game has changed somewhat; we have been going at this from the wrong angle. There was only one intentional victim," he said. "The others were to cover that one up. Our sadly missed friend Doctor Ransom hit the nail on the head when he said that the only link is the fact they were all killed by the same person, to paraphrase him.

"One of the victims was murdered for a reason; the others - Ransom included - were to cover up that reason. To confuse us, to make us think there is a link where none exists. They were random killings." This was met by excited murmurs. "Now," he said over the rising volume. "We have to find out which one was intentional – and I *do* include Doctor Ransom in that.

"I want to know if anyone had reason to murder any of our victims.

"Mills, you take Quinn. McGuire you take Ransom, you'll need a lot of help with him. Chatris, you take Patterson," he groaned. "Got a problem with that, Chatris?"

"It's not likely to be her, is it sir?"

"We don't know yet, do we, Sergeant? She may have stolen a friend's boyfriend and her friend is a bit unhinged or hormonal." Someone said "inbred" in a stage whisper. "Quite. Cotteril and I will take Prentice. Now get on with it."

Standing on the doorstep at 23, The Willows, Cotteril looked out of the corner of his eye at his superior. He definitely had a smug look on his face.

The door opened and Mrs Prentice took a small step back as she took in who was there. "Inspector, what a surprise," she said, then turned to the younger man. "And Sergeant Cotteril, isn't it?" He nodded. "Please come in." She stood aside to let them pass.

Scott Prentice was lounging across a settee. He sat up quickly on seeing the policemen, a look on his face that in an earlier, less enlightened age would have had him swinging from the gallows.

"Do sit down," she said. "Scott, be a love and get the inspector and the sergeant a drink. Tea or coffee?"

"We're fine thank you, madam."

She sat forward. "I do hope you're going to tell us you have caught him," she said expectantly.

Greenwold shook his head slowly. "I'm sorry, not yet. We just need to clear up a few things now that you've had time to think."

He took out his notebook and consulted it. "You said you were expecting Mr Prentice home but was not surprised when you hadn't heard him arrive?"

"Yes. As I told you, we occupied separate rooms and he was usually very considerate if I had gone to bed, and made very little noise." She smiled at the memory.

"What do you do in the evenings while Mr Prentice works late?"

She looked quite taken aback. "Why?

"Just routine, madam."

"What difference would it make what I do? Besides I've already told you once."

He just smiled ingratiatingly. "Ah yes," he said, looking at his notebook. "You go to keep-fit two evenings a week, what about the other evenings?"

"I like the cinema and often go with a friend to see a film then on for a meal. Apart from that, nothing, I stay at home and listen to music or the radio."

"And your friend would be?"

"Oh, no one in particular. There are a few that I go out with on occasion, but no one regularly."

"I see. Had you gone out that evening?"

She shook her head. "No. Not that evening. The night before, Joyce - she lives next door at number 25 - and I had been out to the wine bar in town. Why?"

"So you were home all evening?"

"Yes. I watched television then retired early with a book. Oh, between ten and eleven I would say, although I can't be sure."

Greenwold stood, "Thank you, madam. Sorry to have troubled you. Sir," he said, nodding to Scott, "we'll see ourselves out. Good-day."

In his car, Cotteril could contain himself no longer. "What was all that about, sir?"

"Infidelity, Sergeant. What is sauce for the gander apparently is of no interest to the goose. We know Mr MacAllistair has a yearning for Mrs Prentice, but it seems unrequited."

"To MacAllistair's?" he asked.

"Correct, Sergeant."

They were shown straight in and MacAllistair sprang from his chair to greet them.

"Any news?" he asked eagerly.

"Our investigations are continuing," Greenwold said stuffily.

"So none then."

Greenwold ignored the remark. "We've just come from Mrs Prentice, she seems to be coping well."

"Yes, a very strong woman. Very much her own woman as well."

"And very attractive, sir."

MacAllistair looked flustered, as if Greenwold had just told a very dirty joke.

"Quite."

"How long had you known of Mr Prentice's, shall we say, other interests, sir?"

"Oh," he looked decidedly uncomfortable. "Yes, that. Well, it was a shock I can tell you. I suppose I knew quite a while ago but wasn't sure until he told me. Must be, oh, four, maybe five years."

The inspector shook his head. "Four or five years?" He flipped through his notebook. "I'm sure you said six months the last time we met."

"What? Oh, yes. The latest one is six months or so, I'm not sure exactly, but he had strayed before."

"I see. And you and Mrs Prentice…"

He gave a hollow laugh, "Not for the want of trying, Inspector." He sighed, "Helen is… I felt that as Brian…" he looked flustered. "Oh I don't know what I mean to say, Inspector."

"Did you tell Mrs Prentice of Mr Prentice?"

"No!" The indignation was vehement. "I would never stoop so low. I really don't know how Helen became aware, but then again she does … did, live with him. She must have known, women's intuition is not to be sniffed at, Inspector."

"No, sir. So you decided to bide your time?"

"Yes, I suppose you could say that. I did try to wean myself off Helen, as it were, but it was no use."

"You *are* a married man, sir?"

He sighed again. "Yes, yes I am married." He put his head in his hands and after a moment looked up, his eyes red. "Do you know what it's like to be in the grip of something, a habit, an obsession? That even though you know you are risking everything, your work, your home, your marriage, you just can't let it go.

"Mary, my wife, is a wonderful, warm, loving person, Inspector. If I left it would destroy her but…"

Greenwold wanted to drag him from the pit he was sliding into. "Did you make your feelings known to Mrs Prentice?"

"Yes," he paused, then laughed, just once. "She was mortified. If I had said I was a child molester it couldn't have received a worse reception."

"And yet?"

"Yes, and yet. And yet I couldn't let go. So I let Brian continue with his dalliances, even helped him by turning a blind eye, in the hope Helen would come to her senses and split from him."

"Falling into your arms," the inspector finished the thought for him. He just looked extremely guilty and embarrassed.

"I suppose I should seek some professional help." What started a declaration faltered and became a plea for help, as if not sure of the best course to take.

"That would be best, sir."

"Does Mary... I mean does she..."

"No sir, that won't be necessary." The officers stood. "Thank you for your candour, sir. We will see ourselves out."

"You think MacAllistair did it?" Cotteril said as they drove to the apartment where Katie and her brother lived.

"Why would I think that, Sergeant?"

"He's obsessed with Mrs Prentice, capable of anything." Greenwold nodded. "Prentice is stealing off him to keep his bit on the side." He winced at the euphemism. "All in all it would be better if Prentice met with an accident leaving the way clear for big Mac."

"And there you have it," Greenwold said enigmatically.

"Have what?"

"Why he couldn't have done it."

"I don't follow."

"Big Mac, you said it yourself." Cotteril's face was a blank. "Think of the video of poor Emily. How tall would you say she was?"

"Five-four, five-five."

"Correct, and the assailant?"

Cotteril's mouth formed an "O". "About two inches taller."

"And Mac is…"

"Big. Over six foot. So why…?"

"To answer some of the questions, Sergeant."

They pulled up at the gatehouse to Drover Way. The guard, recognising them, waved them through. "And now we're going to answer a few more."

Stephen opened the door and immediately looked concerned.

"Oh, hello, um, come in won't you?" They went through to the lounge; there was no sign of Katie. "Do you have any news?"

"Sorry sir. Just a few more questions if I may?"

"Of course."

"Is Miss Watkins here?"

"I'm sorry; she's in town shopping. Can I help?"

Greenwold had been wandering around the room; a dresser that had photographs on had caught his eye. He picked one up and studied it then turned back to Stephen. "Yes, sir. Thank you." He replaced the photo and continued. "The night of the incident, at what time did Mr Prentice arrive?"

"Just after seven I think. I came in after he had arrived. Katie could give you a better idea."

"Do you know if Mrs Prentice had any idea what was going on?"

"I would say she certainly did know, Inspector. You see, Brian came clean with her. Told her everything."

"I see."

"But she wanted to cling on, for the sake of the children."

"But they're adults," Cotteril chipped in.

"Yes, damn expensive adults," he said, suddenly angry. "They were the original spoiled brats, still are."

"You are very close to your sister, sir?"

"Yes, Katie and I are very close. Our mother died a few

153

years ago, we never knew our father. We only have each other now."

"Well thank you, sir, you've been very helpful."

"Not at all, Inspector. Should I call you when Katie gets back?"

"No, there's no need for that, sir. If we need to talk to her we'll come back, but that's all for now."

"I assume they're not under suspicion?" Cotteril asked when they were back in the car.

"No. I would have thought he, or his sister for that matter, would be more likely to kill Mrs Prentice rather than Mr Prentice, wouldn't you?"

"Yes sir. Mind you…"

"Yes?"

"Well, he fits the build of the assailant. He's taller I know, but he could have been crouching or the angle of the camera…"

"Cast it from your mind, Sergeant. It wasn't him."

Chapter 24

DS Mills pulled up outside the offices where David Quinn had spent his days. His wife and her girlfriend had already been eliminated, they had no reason to want him dead and the sad little lady friend was the same - she had a vested interest in keeping him alive, she could hear wedding bells.

The offices proudly boasted "Cyntex Systems" on the glass revolving doors. He pushed through them and walked up to the reception desk.

"Can I help you, sir?" a smartly dressed young lady asked. He showed his warrant card. "Oh!"

"Would you let Mr Stanley know I am here please, he is expecting me."

She dialled a number and passed on Mills' message, hung up and asked him to take a seat, someone would be down directly.

He cast his eyes around while he was waiting. Awards adorned the walls, totally meaningless to all but those in this line of business. The glass coffee table held some journals and daily papers - the Times and the FT.

"Would you like a coffee while you're waiting? It is fresh brewed."

"No thank you."

She looked slightly offended but went back to her computer screen.

Shortly afterwards, a man in his late thirties breezed into reception and walked over to the sergeant.

"Detective Sergeant Mills I presume?" He held out a hand in greeting. Mills stood and shook it. "Won't you please come this way." He led him to a meeting room just the other side of reception. There were two other men and a woman already in the room. "Allow me to introduce everyone," he said.

"This is Jane Ridgely; she was Mr Quinn's business co-ordinator." Mills nodded to her as she was too far away to shake hands. "And this is Stephen Buyers, Mr Quinn's immediate manager." He stepped round the table and shook Mills' hand. "This is Trevor Standish, Mr Quinn's department manager, and you know who I am. Everybody, this is Detective Sergeant Mills. Won't you please sit down?"

They all took their seats and Mills got the distinct impression the tables had been turned, he was being interviewed instead of doing the interviewing.

"I thought it best to get all those you might want to meet together once I received your call this morning."

"Thank you, that's very helpful, sir." He took out his notebook and pen. "Did Mr Quinn work closely with any of you? On a daily basis I mean?"

Everyone looked at Jane Ridgeley, a smartly dressed woman in her forties, a bit hard looking but not unattractive.

"Mr Quinn worked mainly autonomously. I used to look after his diary and arrange meetings, but apart from that he worked pretty much alone." She had a clear, clipped way of speaking as if giving instructions.

"Was there anyone in particular that he used to spend the time of day with? Around the coffee machine maybe, or at lunch time?"

"He was very insular. The divorce had hit him hard; apparently his wife had run off with another man." Close, Mills thought, but no cigar.

"I'm sure the sergeant doesn't want tittle-tattle, keep to the facts please, Jean." Stanley reproached her.

"Sorry. He used to be fairly easy going but after the divorce he withdrew. All he wanted to do was get on with his work, then go home."

"Did anyone visit Mr Quinn during the week leading up to his death?"

Jane blanched at the mention of the "D" word but recovered. "Yes, he had three appointments in the week before…"

"Do you have a list of who they were with?"

"Yes." She opened an A4 sized diary in front her, slipped on the tiniest pair of glasses Mills had ever seen, and read. "There was Steven Harkin from Dorson's on Monday; they are an art house we use for promotions and flyers. A Mr Dwyer from the advertising agency; they place our adverts in the industry journals that you may have seen in reception." She turned a few pages and continued, "And … Oh! There doesn't appear to be a name, but they were from MacAllistair and Prentice." She looked perplexed while Mills struggled to remain impassive. "That is most unusual for Mr Quinn not to follow procedure."

"You see, Sergeant, all visitors have to be registered with reception before they arrive, a security procedure we have. Some of the work we do is quite sensitive and we can't have just anyone wandering around," Stanley supplied.

"You say it was MacAllistair and Prentice? Did you see the person yourself?"

"No, I'm afraid not."

"Did this person sign in at reception?"

"It's all on-line. Even the visitor passes are generated from the system."

"Can we see the entry for this visitor?"

"I'll see what I can do," Buyers said and left the room.

"Mr Standish," Mills turned to the other man, "how was Mr Quinn regarded in the company?"

He shrugged, "A solid worker, very diligent. Always willing

to help. A team player up until the divorce," he added. "I don't know of anyone who had a bad word to say about him."

Buyers returned with a laptop and plugged a lead into a port at the end of the desk. He watched the screen while everyone else in the room watched him, with the exception of Mills who was taking the opportunity to study everyone.

Why the reception committee, he wondered. It's as if they're working to a script, making sure no one says anything out of turn.

"Here we go," Buyers said at last. "Let's see now. It was a Miss, sorry, Ms Brolin of MacAllistair and Prentice. She signed in at ten-thirty and out again at twelve o'clock." He looked up from the screen.

"I remember now," Jane chipped in. "She wasn't his usual contact there. They went out to lunch together."

"Do you have a description of her?"

"I'm afraid not. I didn't see her, only the entry in the visitors' booking system. Someone called for Mr Quinn at, I think it was one-thirty, and seemed quite put out, as if he had been expecting Mr Quinn to have called him earlier." Mills noted all this down. There was a silence while he did so but the police are good at silences; it's amazing what people will say just to fill the gap. He deliberately took his time.

"I believe I saw her," Buyers said. "She was quite short and neatly dressed. She had an open top car. A Mazda or something like that. I remember because my wife had been pestering me for one and I was admiring it when they both got in."

"Any idea of her age?"

"Sorry. Totally useless in that department. Could've been thirty, or maybe forty but not a young girl."

"How did they seem together? Did they look like business associates or something more?"

"I've no idea how I would be able to tell. Business associates at a guess."

158

"I suppose there is no means of knowing where they went? He didn't mention it when he got back?"

Jane shook her head. "I didn't see him the rest of the day."

"Last question: How was Mr Quinn doing in his job here? Was he in line for promotion, or maybe the opposite?" Ah, bull's-eye. The swift glance from Buyers to Standish told him all he needed to know.

Standish spoke up, "Actually, Sergeant, he hadn't been doing very well recently and we had had to talk to him about it. He wasn't in fear for his job, not yet. But he certainly had to look to his laurels and get back on track."

"Well thank you very much for your help," Mills said, standing and pocketing his notebook. He shook hands all round and left a few business cards.

As he walked out, he turned to Miss Ridgeley. "Did he have any favourite haunts for lunch?"

She thought a while, her lips pressed together. "I think the Greyhound on the West Road. He mentioned it once or twice, said they did good food there."

"Thank you again," and this time, quieter, he said, "If I need to call on you later, what is your home address?"

"Oh," she looked a little flustered. "Well, it's 139, Curtis Crescent."

"Thank you."

Mills nodded to the receptionist on his way out and climbed into his car. He didn't immediately drive off. He knew they would be watching from the window and he wanted to make them sweat a little. He certainly intended to talk to Miss Ridgeley again. He felt the men, Standish in particular, were holding her back.

He read through his notes; he needed to get some idea of the relationship with the mystery woman, a visit to the Greyhound may help there, but first he called in to Inspector Greenwold regarding the MacAllistair and Prentice connection.

"Sir, it appears there could have been a connection between Quinn and Prentice," he said once he had been patched through. "Quinn dealt with the company MacAllistair and Prentice and was visited by someone from there shortly before his demise." He listened as Greenwold told him to get over there and follow it up. "Yes sir." He hung up, pulled away sharply and headed toward the High Street.

"I am Detective Sergeant Mills of Perry Green CID. Could I see Mr MacAllistair please?" he asked the receptionist.

"I'm sorry sir, but he's visiting a client. Could anybody else help you?"

"I'm actually looking for Ms Brolin, is she in?"

"I'll see sir." She typed at the computer, and then dialled. "Ms Brolin? There's a gentleman to see you in reception, a Detective Sergeant Mills." She listened on her headset; it must have deafened her because Mills could hear the funk Ms Brolin was getting in. Eventually she said thank you and hung up. "She will be down directly, sir, if you would like to take a seat."

DS Mills sat and looked around the reception area; more incomprehensible awards, more trade journals and, of course, the Times and the FT.

He was browsing the Times when he heard Ms Brolin clip-clopping across the tiled floor to meet him. She held out her hand. "Sylvia Brolin."

"DS Mills. Thank you for seeing me, there are just a few questions I would like to ask you. Is there somewhere we can go a bit more private?"

"Through here." She led the way through a door and down a corridor to a small office. Once they were seated she said, "I'm sure I don't know what you could want with me, Inspector."

"That's Sergeant, madam."

"Sorry. Sergeant. Is it to do with poor Mr Prentice? If it is, I hardly knew him."

"No, it isn't about Mr Prentice. Do you know a man called David Quinn?"

She looked taken aback. "Err, yes. Yes I do. In fact I was expecting to meet with him later in the week. Why?"

"Did you visit him," he looked in his notebook, "last Thursday?"

"Yes. We had a meeting then went to lunch. Has something happened to Mr Quinn?"

"Where did you go for lunch?"

"The Greyhound, it's a favourite of David's."

David's, Mills noticed. Not "his" or "Mr Quinn's" but "David's". "At what time did you return?"

"Oh, about three, three-thirty. Why do you ask?"

"Bear with me, madam. Did you use your car or his?"

"Mine. It was a lovely day so we had the top down."

"And you dropped him back at his work after lunch?"

"Yes, no! Actually, no I didn't. He asked me to drop him in town, at the top of the High Street."

"And this was between three and three-thirty you say?"

"Yes."

"How did Mr Quinn seem to you? Was he agitated, worried, withdrawn?"

"He was his normal self. Not a great conversationalist but good company all the same. He listens very attentively."

"Excuse me for asking this but was your relationship with Mr Quinn purely business?"

She blushed and tilted her head down. "No." DS Mills kept quiet. She took a deep breath. "We have been seeing one another for a month now. He's divorced you know, and I'm… well I'm separated from my husband. We aren't living together or anything like that. It hasn't got that far, yet," she added.

"How often did you see Mr Quinn out of office hours?"

"Look, this is all getting a bit personal. What do you want to know for? Is David in trouble? What's happened?"

He closed his notebook and lowered his voice. "I'm sorry to have to tell you but Mr Quinn was found outside his flat last Thursday, he had been murdered."

He watched her intently; the shock, then absorbing what he had said, then the tears. Oh God, the tears. He took a clean handkerchief from his pocket and passed it to her.

"How?" she croaked.

"He had been stabbed."

"Oh no! No! Poor David. Oh God!" She cried bitterly for some minutes then gradually calmed down and gained control. Through sniffs she said, "What has happened to his…"

"He is still at the mortuary. We had to do an autopsy. Standard procedure in a suspicious death."

"Have you any idea who did it?"

"We are following several lines of inquiry. I was hoping maybe you could help. Is there anyone you know who might wish to harm Mr Quinn?"

"Oh no. No. He was such a nice man. A bit broken up about his marriage but everybody liked him."

"Did you meet regularly?"

"Twice a week, sometimes three. But usually twice."

"Any particular days?"

"Yes, we had all Saturday together and Wednesday evenings."

"Do you know what he did the other days?"

There was what DS Mills' mum called a pregnant pause. "No?" she said cautiously, wondering what was coming next. But Mills didn't follow it up.

"Did you meet any of his other friends? Did he introduce you to anyone?"

"No," she said a in a small voice. "No one. I thought… As

he was recently divorced I didn't give it a thought." DS Mills smiled reassuringly.

"Thank you. I'm sorry to be the bearer of such bad news. We will let you know when his body is released but I would expect his ex-wife would make the funeral arrangements." He stood then and looked back at her; she looked very small and vulnerable now. "Is there someone I can call for you?"

She looked up. "No. I'll be fine. Thank you." She smiled bravely.

He turned and left the room, closing the door quietly behind him.

Chapter 25

DS Chatris pulled up outside the Patterson residence and sat for a while listening to Classic FM on the radio. He felt he had drawn the short straw in that Emily was the least likely target for murder he had ever heard of. He switched the radio off as the announcer came back on, and stepped out of his car.

The door was opened by a red-eyed Mr Patterson who obviously had had very little sleep. He stood aside to let the sergeant through on seeing his warrant card.

The living room was in near darkness as the curtains were drawn. Mrs Patterson was sitting on the sofa staring into space; she also looked as if she had not slept in days.

"I'm sorry to have to intrude again but we need to ask you some questions about Emily," he said as gently as he could. At the mention of her daughter's name, Mrs Patterson came back to the present.

"Yes Sergeant. Of course, anything we can do…"

He took a deep breath. "Do you know of anyone that Emily may have fallen out with recently?"

"Oh no!" she was genuinely shocked at the question. "Emily was loved by everyone. She was a very popular girl both at school and the neighbourhood."

"But the fact that she is popular can cause some resentment?" he tried.

She looked to her husband for support; he just shook his head.

"Nothing like that. She was loved by everyone."

"Did Emily have a boyfriend?"

"Not to our knowledge. She was more interested in her studies and getting good results than having silly liaisons with boys." There was something in her tone that made the sergeant want to pursue this further, but not with the parents.

"Do you know her circle of friends?"

"Yes. We've had them all round here at some time or another. We always said this house was their second form room. Do you know, sometimes, if Emily was out when they arrived, they would come in anyway and talk to us until she got back. They were all very nice and charming, and they felt quite at home here. We were very pleased about that."

"Could you name her friends?" A quizzical gaze met his question. "So I can be sure we have interviewed everyone who had contact with Emily," he explained.

Mrs Patterson sighed, "We will write a list for you, Sergeant." Mr Patterson stood to get a pen and paper.

"While you're doing that, would you mind if I had a look round Emily's room?"

"No, not at all. The other policemen have already been through her things but if you want to, that's fine by us."

He thanked her and made his way unescorted up the stairs. At the top, the landing gave on to five rooms. The bathroom and toilet had the usual soaps and lotions on the sides and in the cupboards. There was a room set aside for, he assumed, a study as it was dominated by a large computer desk and had various posters and maps on the walls and a large office calendar with various adhesive shapes dotted over it. The day of the murder had a green star stuck to it and the name "Bohemia" in green ink underneath. He scanned it for names or initials and came up with SW written very lightly in pencil several times in the last month and a half as if someone wanted to be reminded but didn't want anyone else to know what about.

The master bedroom had an unmade bed and bedside tables strewn with various pills and potions. Some prescribed, some herbal, all useless he suspected. He idly went through the bedside cupboard on both sides of the bed, nothing untoward there.

Emily's room was bright and airy with everything in its place. A row of cuddly toys perched along the pillow waiting for their owner. It made him feel uncomfortable, as if they were watching his every move.

He made a meticulous search of the room and finally found what he was looking for, a diary. It had been stuffed inside one of the toys, her secret hiding place. A shiver went down his spine as he retrieved it. "Sorry, Emily, love," he said, feeling almost that she were there looking over his shoulder. He flicked through it quickly, she had been an avid chronicler, and every page was filled with her neat handwriting.

He stood in the doorway and looked around the room one more time. He stopped as he saw a toy perched on top of the wardrobe all by itself. It didn't fit with the rest of the room. Everything was so deliberate and symmetrical, yet this toy looked as if it had been hurriedly shoved there. He took it down and squeezed it; he felt the hard shape of yet another book in its intestines. He looked the toy over for an obvious opening but could not find one. Then he noticed that if you squeezed the neck in a certain way, the mouth opened wider and he could see the book inside.

He put the toy back and flicked through this book. It had the same neat writing but with less on each page, and this time in red. He pocketed both books and left the room.

The last room was obviously that of a teenage boy. A guitar sat on its stand in the corner; posters of Van Halen and Guns 'N Roses adorned the walls. A hi-fi and wide-screen television and a bed almost lifted off the ground by the magazines and other articles shoved under it.

He drew out a stack of the magazines, the usual fare: FHM, Guitarist, and Viz and some more salacious items hidden among them. He sat back on his haunches and pondered. He had never heard mention of a brother. He was sure there was nothing on the board in the incident room and he hadn't seen another person around the house.

He stood and went back downstairs to the living room to where Mr and Mrs Patterson had just finished the list. It was long, he noticed with a feeling of doom. All were potential interviewees.

"That's all we can remember, Sergeant," Mr Patterson said, handing the list over. "Her friends at school may know of more."

"Thank you. Tell me, did Emily have a brother?" A look passed between them and Mr Patterson sat at his wife's side as if reassuring her. "I noticed the other bedroom. The door was open a little," he explained.

"Yes. Yes of course," Mr Patterson said. "David. He is … not here."

"We don't know where he is," Mrs Patterson blurted out. "He went off six months ago and we haven't heard anything since. He should be here. He has to know." She turned, imploring eyes on the sergeant. "Could you find him? Tell him to come home. Tell him what has happened?"

"You say he left six months ago, any indication where he may have gone? Friends or names he may have mentioned?"

A resigned expression came to Mr Patterson's face. "He got in with a bad lot. Hoodlums. Going to rock concerts and raves, sometimes we wouldn't see him for days on end then he'd turn up, broke as usual."

"Do you know the names of these individuals? Something we could start with?"

He shook his head sadly, "Only that they met up in that pub near the park."

"The Green Man?"

"That's it. A real dive."

Sergeant Chatris could only agree with him. The Green Man had a well-deserved reputation and had been raided on numerous occasions over the years.

"Thank you sir, madam." They both saw him out. "I'll see if we can track down your son and make sure he knows what has happened." At the door he turned as if suddenly thinking of something. "Did they get on? David and Emily?"

Mrs Patterson was horrified, "You can't possibly suspect…"

"No, no. I'm not saying that. It's just that he may know more of Emily's acquaintances."

"Oh, I see." She calmed down. "Yes, they got on very well. I told you, everyone loved Emily," and she started to weep quietly; her husband put his arm around her shoulders and with a shrug took her back to the living room.

At his desk, Sergeant Chatris read through Emily's diary. It was the usual adolescent stuff - friends and what she thought of them, who was going out with who and, more recently, who had got more concerned with sex and who said they had "done it" and who hadn't. He got the impression young Emily was an innocent.

But the second book put all that into perspective. It was as if someone else had written it, but it was clearly Emily's handwriting. It was a notebook whereas the other was a diary. It wasn't dated, it just had blocks of writing, and what writing! Far from innocent, this was stronger than anything he had seen under young David's bed.

She detailed meetings with men, or just one man, he couldn't decide which. Where they met, where they went, what they did – all in graphic detail. There was the mention of "photo-shoots" in hotels; he couldn't believe what he was reading. It was all there, nothing left to the imagination.

The men, or man, in the book were older than her - that was certain. Just how much older was never revealed.

He sat back, dumbfounded. Could the man in these writings have become nervous about Emily's ability to keep their meetings a secret? Could he have found out that she had documented everything? Was he someone in a position of trust, say a teacher or another parent? In short, could he have a motive for murder? One thing was for sure, he needed to find out who he, or they, were. Maybe there was a connection to the initials SW that he had seen on her calendar.

He commandeered one of the detective constables and had him tracking down the whereabouts of David Patterson while he left for the school to talk to some of Emily's closer friends. He was hopeful that at least one might be aware of Emily's exploits.

As he sat in Miss Harmsworth's office at Eversholt School waiting for the girls to be rounded up, he asked about whether she knew if the girls had regular boyfriends.

"Oh I'm sure some of them do. We give them quite early instruction in sex education, knowing they will at some point find themselves in a situation with a young lad. I just hope the girls would do the right thing."

The sergeant wasn't quite sure what "the right thing" was as far as Miss Harmsworth was concerned and never got to find out as the girls arrived at that point.

"This is Penny Abrahams and Collette Jones. Your Detective Inspector Greenwold has already interviewed them."

"Yes I know. I'm sorry, girls, but I need to ask you a few more questions about Emily. Is that all right?" They both nodded dumbly.

"Perhaps you wouldn't mind waiting outside, Miss Harmsworth?" She looked a little put out but complied. He had primed her that what he had to ask the girls may not be forthcoming if she were in the room. Although she put up strong objections, she agreed they could be seen without her in attendance as long as she was stationed outside the door.

"How often did Emily go to the Bohemia nightclub?"

"It was only her third time," Collette answered. "She had just turned eighteen a few weeks ago; she couldn't get in before that because they card you at the door." The sergeant didn't need telling that "carding" meant providing proof of being over eighteen.

"But I'm sure intelligent girls like you found ways around that, didn't you?" They looked at one another but said nothing. "You won't get in trouble if you tell me you went there when you were under age. We are willing to overlook that in view of the situation." Again they looked at each other, this time Penny spoke up.

"We had been there before, about three months ago. We got fake IDs from someone we know."

"Yeah but Emily didn't get in," Collette cut in.

"No. They wouldn't believe her."

"Or Joanne," Collette chimed in again.

"So they went to the pub."

"We were already in there before they got stopped, you see."

"How about boyfriends?" the sergeant asked. "We know she was seeing someone," he lied.

After a pause Collette said, "Emily didn't have a boy…" and left it hanging as Penny gave her a warning look. The sergeant sat forward in his seat, lowering his voice.

"We found her notebook in her bedroom," he said simply. They looked at one another, not understanding. Oh damn, he thought. Maybe I've got this wrong, maybe she hadn't told them. He pressed on, "The book where she kept a record of her "dates" with someone older than her."

"Eh?" Penny asked. He took the notebook out of his pocket and placed it on the table between them. They both stared at it, and then they burst out laughing - not exactly what he had expected.

"What's the joke girls?"

"That?" Penny laughed. "You want to know about that?"

"Yes. I'd be very interested to know about what is in this book." He felt irritated that they found it so amusing.

They looked at each other again and both went to pockets in their jackets and pulled out similar notebooks with similar red writing.

"Have you ever seen those "erotic novels" the book shops sell?" Collette asked rhetorically. "Well we thought we could do better."

"Yes, then it became a competition. You know, who could write the juiciest stuff," Penny butted in.

"There's loads of us got them, not just Emily and us."

"So they're all fiction?" he asked, feeling foolish.

"Of course they are," Penny laughed. "We'd never do anything like that." They both pulled faces and said, "Yuk!" and laughed.

"We stole one of those books from Smith's in the High Street," Collette said.

"To see what they're like," Penny interjected. He was getting used to their double-act by now.

"It was disgusting."

"Yeah but we thought, why not? Let's have a go and see if we could do better."

"Yeah, it was just us three."

"And Simone," Penny corrected.

"Oh yeah, and Simone who started it, but it caught on."

"Now everyone's doing it. Well, nearly everyone in our year."

"It's just a bit of fun," Collette concluded.

Sergeant Chatris closed his notebook and picked up Emily's from the table. "Thank you very much, that is a weight off my mind," he smiled.

"God! You must have thought terrible things about poor Emily," Penny said, realising how it must have seemed. "We didn't mean anything by it."

"I know. And I'm grateful for you being so honest with me. It has saved a lot of wasted effort." He stood and saw them to the door. "Just one last thing," he said, as they were about to leave. "Do the initials SW mean anything to you?" They looked at one another then shook their heads. "Thank you for your help," and he held the door open for them. They both looked back at him and waved, a little embarrassed, as they walked back to class.

Chapter 26

"Bloody typical," DS McGuire said as he surveyed what must have once been a dining room but now looked like a lost property office. "All these bleedin' head doctors are the messiest buggers you ever come across."

As they had driven up the road to Doctor Ransom's house, they had been quietly impressed with the neighbourhood. Nice semi-detached houses with long, well kept front lawns, cars in the driveway, all shining as if they had just been valeted. The doctor's house was just as neat and orderly as the rest, the only difference being there was no car. But the illusion was soon dispelled as they walked through the front door. Books lined the stairs, naked bulbs in the sockets. This was a house where the occupant merely thought of it as shelter and little more.

"What are we looking for, Sarge?" DC Potten asked as he knocked over a tower of papers that sprouted from the floor like an origami rubber plant.

"Case notes." This was met by a hollow laugh from the detective constable. "Yes, I know." He stood, hands on hips, or rather where his hips should be if they were not covered by "love handles" that hung like saddle-bags over the too tight trousers. "Like looking for a haystack on a needle."

"We gotta read all these?"

"That's the general idea. To see if there's any of his… clients," he chose the word carefully; he would have preferred "nutters", "that would be predisposed to doing away with him and covering it by bumping off three other poor unfortunates first."

"It'll take a lifetime," Potten moaned as he tried to reconstruct the tower of files.

"Ours is not to reason why. Ours is but to do, while all the other buggers swan around solving the case before we've finish," he said dejectedly. "Let's box all this up and get it back to the station. Perhaps we'll catch some poor unsuspecting DCs and plods hanging around and rope them in."

While Potten assembled boxes and piled the files and papers into them, DS McGuire wandered around the rest of the house. He felt he had been unfair to the good doctor; the rest of the house was fairly tidy, for a given value of tidy that is. If it were to be compared to McGuire's estranged wife's house, it was a tip. But compared to McGuire's house… Well, there's nothing wrong with a little haphazardness, he thought. Shows character.

A patrol car pulled up outside and the two PCs came up the path as McGuire opened the door. "Thanks for your help, lads, it's through there." He had had the foresight to book a local patrol car to come over to help with ferrying what he expected to be copious amounts of books and the like, and he congratulated himself on being a shrewd judge.

He stepped outside and lit a cigarette. It was so quiet here. He looked up and down the road, nothing was moving. No cars or people, just the birds in the trees that were planted every fifty yards or so along the roadside. An aircraft passed over and he watched it glinting in the sunlight as it turned south, heading for some holiday destination.

DC Potten came out of the house carrying two of the boxes as he ground the cigarette underfoot. "Much more?" he asked, more out of embarrassment than the desire to know.

"Yeah, plenty if you feel like lending a hand," he said, dumping the boxes on the driveway and searching his pockets for the keys. McGuire ambled over to the car and hefted one of the boxes into the tailgate as Potten laid the back seats down.

He picked a file at random off the top of the box and leafed through it. Blowing air from puffed cheeks he said, "It's gonna be a bugger reading that lot. His handwriting's nearly as bad as mine."

DC Potten straightened up and arched his back. "How will we know?"

"What?"

"If one of these "cases" is the perp."

McGuire raised an inquisitive eyebrow. "The what?"

"The perp. The perpetrator of the crime. Perp."

"You've been watching too much CSI Miami, perp indeed. In answer to your question, how the hell should I know, I'm just a working Dick." He threw the file back into the box.

"Three bloody hours," he said to anyone who would listen. "Three bloody hours it took to get all that stuff boxed. We had to make two journeys in both cars, there's mountains of the bloody stuff."

He was standing in the doorway of the office he had commandeered for the purpose of storing the files. The idea being that two or three uniformed officers could work there going through it all leaving him free to "get amongst the action" as he put it. Now he realised he had badly underestimated the immensity of the job - you couldn't even fit one person in the office with it all, let alone two or three. "I need a drink," he said, turning away. He went to close the door but as it opened inwards, it was now trapped behind a chest-high pile of boxes. "Who's gonna nick it anyway," he said as he turned away and walked down the corridor in search of tea.

His luck was in, at the drinks machine he rounded up four uniformed police to help before they went off duty.

"Just a little light reading," he lied then led them to the office. "Take a box each, go through it looking for…" he opened his pocket book, grunted, put it away again and searched the rest of his pockets unsuccessfully before telling them to look for any patient who sounded dodgy. He then made his getaway before they realised that every one of the patients was dodgy, or they wouldn't have been patients.

"Any luck?" Inspector Greenwold asked as McGuire entered the incident room. It was amazingly quiet.

"No. I reckon we're on a hiding to nothing with Doc. My money's on the wife."

"Which one?"

"The first." He sat and put his feet up on the desk, but took them down again in the heat of Greenwold's glare.

"Explain," he said, pulling up a chair.

"Ok. The way I see it is, keep it simple. It invariably is. She, the first one."

"Prentice."

"Yeah, Prentice. Well she gets the arse with hubby over his dalliance with the lovely Katie and one night decides to do something about it, permanently." Greenwold couldn't help noticing he had no problem remembering Katie's name.

"Go on."

"She sees after a while we're at a bit of a loss and thinks, hang on, that was easy. If I bump a few more off, they'll not know whether they're coming or going. So she buys a new knife and repeats the act, each time it gets easier." He sat back, a smug grin on his face.

Greenwold nodded admiringly. "Not bad," he admitted. "But why not just divorce Mr Prentice? A lot less messy and no risk."

McGuire studied his rotund abdomen, his lips pursed in thought. He nodded, "Quite right. Don't make sense. But then, when has killing ever made sense, eh?"

"True," the inspector agreed. "But unless there is a motive we're just not seeing, I don't buy it."

McGuire sat up straight. "Want me to dig around?" he asked hopefully.

"Don't you have some paperwork to catch up on?"

"Oh come on, sir, I did come up with the idea. Let me see it through even if it is a dead-end, at least it'll eliminate her." He put on his most earnest face. "I'll go mental if I have to look at another nut-job's file. I do my best work out there," he nodded through the window.

"Ok, I'll detail your DC to carry on with the files. You have a fresh look at Mrs Prentice; see what you can dig up. I'll give you two days, then you're back on reading duty."

"Cheers, sir." He flashed a smile and wasted no time in leaving the room to give poor old Potten the good news, he didn't want Greenwold changing his mind.

Something McGuire had said started nagging at the Inspector. He didn't buy his theory at all and thought it was probably the first thing that came into his head to save him having to read those files, but something struck a chord with him.

He looked at the board, mentally putting Mrs Prentice in the middle with a label "prime suspect" under her. After a while he reached out without looking and picked up the telephone receiver.

"Put me though to DS Cotteril, would you?" he said, and then waited patiently to be connected. "Could you come to the incident room please," he said when Cotteril answered. "Quick as you like," and he replaced the receiver on its cradle.

A few minutes later Cotteril burst through the door, a concerned look on his face. "Sir?"

"Tell me what you saw when you searched the Prentices' home."

He sat down and pulled out his notebook. He thumbed through the pages then started to read. "I went upstairs first, while I had the chance to be alone," he explained. Greenwold nodded for him to continue.

"The girl's room was very tidy, a bit too tidy if you know what I mean. Looked like it had been done for her. I couldn't see her doing housework so I suppose they must have someone in to do it. Anyway, she had three double wardrobes, bursting with clothes. All in polythene wraps, all hung neatly, everything in its place.

"She had a diary in her knicker drawer." The Inspector raised an eyebrow and he quickly carried on. "Nothing much, only appointments and details of trips abroad." He looked up, "You wouldn't believe the places she's been," he shook his head. "Talk about globe trotter." He went back to his notebook. "Her jewellery box was full to overflowing as well. Daddy's little girl does very well for herself.

"The lad's room was typical for his age. He's into skiing in a big way; a massive picture of all the ski runs from some resort on his wall and trophies for slalom on a shelf. No diaries or anything of that nature. Not that I expected any.

"The master bedroom was a bit more lived in, if you know what I mean. Nothing untoward there." He turned a page. "Mr Prentice's room was neat and tidy; everything put away, nothing there either. I thought the garage may turn up something but he obviously wasn't much of a mechanic. Not so much as a petrol can or screwdriver set in there. Just gardening stuff."

"Not surprising, he doesn't drive," the inspector interjected.

He closed his notebook. "All in all, not much to report," he said somewhat sadly.

While he had been talking, the inspector had not taken his eyes off the board. Assembling the family from the pictures, thinking about how different they were and yet… "I think we need to have a word with Katie again, Sergeant," he said. "There's something troubling me but I can't put my finger on it. Something I've seen or heard. I'm pretty sure it was at the twins' flat. Come on, let's go."

Chapter 27

Stephen was just coming out the front door as Inspector Greenwold and Sergeant Cotteril arrived. He paused, the door still open, and turned to call to Katie that the police were back.

In the living room Inspector Greenwold looked at the photos on display and a framed poster on the wall depicting ski runs at a resort in the French Alps.

"Do you ski much, miss?"

Katie looked surprised at the question, "Oh, yes, quite a bit but not as much as Stephen. He's the Franz Klammer of the family."

"Sorry?"

"Oh, Katie means the downhill champion from years ago, Inspector. Just her little joke," Stephen explained.

"I see. Do you ski often then, sir?"

"Not as often as I'd like to, but a couple of times a year Katie and I go with some… friends to Deux Alpes in France. There's year round snow there," he explained. Greenwold noticed a slight pause before he said "friends".

"Is it a skiing club you go with?"

"No, just friends of ours." He looked uncomfortable and changed the subject. "So have there been any developments? Anything to tell us?"

"Our investigations are continuing, sir." He picked up a framed photograph from a group on the mantelpiece, which he assumed was ornamental, as he hadn't seen any chimneys atop the buildings in Drover Way. "Are these the friends, sir?"

Stephen came over to him and looked at the photograph as if seeing it for the first time, his face tense. "Yes, Inspector. Brian was in our skiing group.

The photograph showed Stephen and Katie along with Brian Prentice and two other people he couldn't make out because of the snow goggles and woolly hats. They were all on skis, with white lip salve and huge smiles. He replaced it on the mantelpiece to Stephen's obvious relief, and turned to Katie.

"Would you mind if my Sergeant had a look round at all, miss?" Katie looked alarmed at Stephen.

"Erm, is that really necessary, Inspector? Surely you can't suspect either of us of Brian's murder." It was a statement rather than a question.

"Just routine, sir. May we?"

Katie looked again to Stephen who gave a slight nod. "Be our guest," she said.

As Sergeant Cotteril mounted the stairs, Inspector Greenwold sat in an armchair facing Katie.

"How long have you known Mr Prentice, miss?"

"Two years, it is in my statement, Inspector."

He ignored the barb and continued, "And you met where?"

"Skiing actually. We were on holiday, staying at the same hotel as Brian."

"Was he alone?"

She looked to Stephen again then back at the inspector. "His son was with him."

"Scott Prentice?"

"Yes."

"And the relationship started then?"

"Well, no, not exactly. We found out we all live in Perry Green and arranged to meet up for a meal when we got back. It was supposed to be the four of us but, well, ended up just two."

"I see. And you were living, where?"

"Oh, Stephen and I had a two bedroom flat in Argyll Road on a lease. It was getting hellishly expensive and it was hard to get the management to carry out any repairs. They just didn't care and expected us to do it all even though we were paying them for it."

"How long ago did you move in here?"

"Just over a year ago. In the August."

Cotteril returned to the living room, Greenwold stood. "Thank you, miss, and you sir," he said, making for the door. "We may be back should we need to ask some more questions. Please don't leave the area in the meantime."

Stephen looked quite flustered. "But are we suspects, Inspector?" he asked, following the two policemen to the front door.

Inspector Greenwold stopped suddenly and turned to face him. "You will be until I get some straight answers," he told a stunned Stephen. "What is it you are hiding from us?"

Stephen stood, his face radiating innocence. "I'm sure I don't know what you mean, Inspector," he said.

Greenwold turned on his heel and walked out the front door. "Good day, sir, miss."

"Anything of interest, Sergeant?" Greenwold asked as they drove away.

"Not sure, sir," a puzzled expression on his face.

"Well? Don't keep me in suspense."

"I was looking around Katie's room and something struck me as odd.

"She's having this affair with Mr Prentice but the only photo I saw next to her bed was of her and Mr Prentice's son, Scott. Could we have got it wrong? Is it Scott having the affair with her?"

"McGuire found ski memorabilia in Scott's room," the inspector mused.

Silence descended on them as they drove to the station. Inspector Greenwold was deep in thought, so deep Cotteril imagined he had stopped breathing. When they arrived at the car park he seemed to snap out of it and said, "Get the gang together," and got out.

In the incident room there was the usual subdued babble going on and Inspector Greenwold called them to order.

"Ok," he said when he had their attention. "Who has either interviewed or been to the Prentices' home?" He looked around expectantly. A few hands went up.

"Right, let's have it. You first, McGuire."

"Went to the house as instructed and spoke to the wife. A bit of a cold fish, I thought. I still fancy her for the killing, at least of her husband."

"Anything struck you as not as it should be?"

He pondered this, "She's totally obsessed about that girl of theirs. I know some mothers are, you know, but this seems unhealthy."

The inspector pointed to one of the uniformed officers. "You. Anything to add?"

"Only that someone was there with her the night of the murder, sir."

Everyone turned to view the constable. His ears radiated his embarrassment.

"Go on," the inspector prompted.

"I went through the bins, sir. And there was a pizza box with the order sellotaped to the lid. It was for the night of the murder."

"What makes you think it wasn't just for her? Or she'd got it in for when hubby got home?"

"There were two portions of wedges on the order, both eaten. If it'd been for hubby, half would have been thrown."

"Well done, lad. Ten out of ten for observation," the constable glowed with pride, "and minus one hundred for keeping this nugget to yourself," he shouted. He took a deep breath to calm himself down. "Right, who could have been with her? I want all the suspects checked out again, more thoroughly this time. MacAllistair, the daughter, the son, the neighbour, Jack the bleedin' Ripper. All of them. Get to it."

"Wait!" he shouted as they all stood, "Check out the twins as well, tweedle-dee and tweedle-dumber. Were they really at home with Mr Prentice? Or did one of them offer to walk home with him?

"McGuire, over here," he called to the sergeant as he stood to leave.

He ambled over, a suspicious look on his face. "Sir?"

"Did you have a chance to search the place?"

He looked hurt, "Do bears shi…"

"A simple yes would do. Well?"

"No smoking gun there, sir. Or should that be smoking jacket and trouser set." He smiled amiably.

"Eh?" chimed in Sergeant Cotteril. "What was that?"

"The dark-coloured suit as worn by the murderer of course. Warren said it would be dark brown or blue, something like that."

"When?"

"When what?"

"When did Warren say that?"

"When we watched the CCTV video of Emily of course, where were you?" McGuire asked caustically.

"I… I left the room." He turned urgently to Greenwold. "There *was* a suit there. In the wardrobe when I had a look round the first time we visited."

"What?" McGuire and Greenwold chorused.

"In Mrs Prentice's wardrobe. A sort of fake leather suit. I thought it was a bit kinky myself. It was a really dark, dull colour, a sort of blue; you know, royal blue but dull. Darker than…" he stopped.

Greenwold was first to burst into life. "I want a warrant to search the Prentices' house. I want that suit. Well? What are you waiting for?" he roared. Both men leapt as if they had been burned. They all but ran from the room as Greenwold turned to the board. "So, it all starts to take shape," he said.

He drew a line between Scott Prentice and Katie. He drew a dotted line between MacAllistair and Mrs Prentice. He drew another line from Mr Prentice to Katie, could that be it? He wondered. Scott, the drug pusher's dream, cuckolded by daddy, wreaks terrible revenge? Or was Prentice senior set up? Scott must inherit quite a tidy sum…

"Sergeant!" he bellowed at the top of his voice. A few seconds later a constable's head poked cautiously round the door.

"He's with the super, sir. Getting the warrant."

"You'll do then. Go find McGuire. I want to know what was in Mr Prentice's will, if he had one," he added. "Jump to it and I may just think twice about reprimanding you over that pizza box." The head had disappeared before he had finished speaking.

He turned back to the board. "So," he said, tapping his lips lightly with the marker pen. He drew a ring around Stephen and Katie and put a question mark over it. "Did you do it and little sister provided the alibi?" he said. "But why? What would you gain? Are you part of…" he linked Stephen with Scott, "this? The set-up?" He looked again at Mrs Prentice, MacAllistair, Scott and Geraldine.

"Nah!" he said and crossed out MacAllistair. "Wishful thinking. She won't let you near. She's too busy making sure little Geraldine gets the best…" He stopped again. "Constable!" he shouted. The head reappeared. "Go and find Cotteril and tell him to get straight back here." The head disappeared again.

Ten minutes later Cotteril bust through the door. "Should have the warrant in an hour, sir." He seemed out of breath.

"Constable?" Greenwold shouted. The whole body appeared this time.

"Sir?"

"Find out when the bin men come to the Prentices' and if they've been and where they dump their rubbish." He nodded but Greenwold was not finished yet. "Also, get hold of DS Mills. Get him to talk to the Prentices' neighbours. Did she have a bonfire anytime recently? Has she or the son been seen digging the garden? That suit must be somewhere."

"That it sir?" he asked, hoping Greenwold wouldn't think he was being sarcastic.

"Yes. Then report back here, you're my runner, understand?"

"Yes, sir."

"This is a mess, Sergeant," he said. "An unholy mess." He looked as if he was trying to remember something, then it came. "Oh yes, which wardrobe did you see the suit in? Was it Mrs Prentice's or Miss Prentice's, think carefully."

"Mrs Prentice's. Definitely sir. It had one of those plastic bags over it."

"Good. We have to find that suit. We have to have a lever, a way to interrogate Mrs Prentice so that when her fancy lawyer asks about it in court, we have a rational explanation for bringing her in. I don't want any mistakes on this one."

A phone rang at one of the desks. Cotteril picked it up and listened.

"DS Mills, sir." He held the receiver out.

"Yes?" he listened, scowling to himself. "Right. Now go back and ask if anyone saw a second person at the Prentice..." he listened again as Mills had obviously interrupted him. "She was there? They're sure?" Mills voice, sounding like an angry wasp in a jam jar, buzzed in Greenwold's ear. "Good," he said. "Stay there, we'll be over," and he hung up.

"It seems Miss Prentice was at home that night. She bumped into one of the neighbours and was rude to her. See if you can find out where she was the nights of the other killings. Was she where mummy said or was she skulking around somewhere here in Perry Green?"

"What would be her motive, sir?"

"Perhaps Daddy wouldn't buy her a bow-wow. Who knows? But if we start to drive holes in her story, we may get it out of her. While you're at it, where's that warrant? Chase it up will you? I'm heading over to The Willows, Constable!"

A WPC appeared this time. "Sir?"

"Where's whatsisname?"

"PC Gibbons, sir? Not sure."

"Never mind. Get hold of McGuire, tell him to pick up Mr and Miss Watkins in Drovers way and bring them in for further questioning." He turned to Cotteril, "I want them all here, under one roof. In my backyard."

Chapter 28

The driveway of 23, The Willows looked like the overflow car park for the police station. DS Cotteril had to park in the road and they scrunched up to the front door on foot.

Mrs Prentice was standing on the doorstep screaming at the poor police officer in front of her. As she saw Inspector Greenwold approaching she turned her wrath on him.

"What the hell is the meaning of this?" she demanded. "What are all these…" she paused significantly, "*men* doing here?"

"Mrs Prentice, we have a warrant to search these premises and remove any items pertaining to our inquiries." Cotteril handed her the warrant; she promptly tore it up and threw it at him. "We have more," Greenwold said, unperturbed.

He had witnessed a lot of different reactions when people were served with warrants. One memorable occasion the householder ate the warrant and two days later a bag containing the warrant along with a fair amount of faeces arrived at the station. The post room were not amused.

The officers piled into the house and started their search. Mrs Prentice was apoplectic. She roared, she screamed, she tried to stop the men and pounded them with her fists - all to no avail.

A lawyer turned up and asked to see the warrant and received a stream of abuse for chiding Mrs Prentice for tearing it up. He tried in vain to calm her down, explaining that the police were going about their lawful duty after he had examined the pieces Cotteril had collected. She didn't seem convinced.

Shortly after, Mrs Prentice and her two charges were escorted to the police station to "help with Inspector Greenwold's inquiries".

"You've got all the interview rooms occupied," the desk sergeant said when Cotteril requested separate rooms for the Prentice family. "We'll have to evict a couple, where do you suggest we keep them?"

They moved Stephen and Katie into the custody area while Mrs Prentice, Geraldine and Scott were put in the three interview rooms. While they cooled off, as Greenwold succinctly put it, he took Katie to an unused office and Cotteril tried to locate a spare interview recorder. Eventually they got it all together.

"From your statement, you said that Mr Prentice was with you just prior to his death." Sergeant Cotteril took the lead in the questioning while the inspector sat back, his arms folded across his chest as he watched her; she nodded. "Please say yes or no for the tape, Miss Watkins."

"Yes. That is right," she said in a firm voice, annunciating every word clearly.

"Thank you. And you say he left at roughly ten minutes before midnight?"

"Yes."

"When he left, was he alone?"

She looked from Cotteril to Greenwold and back again. "Yes," she said incredulously, wondering where this was leading and not liking what she suspected would be at the end of it.

"So neither Stephen nor yourself left with him? Went for a little walk in the park before retiring?"

"No! He left at ten to twelve; we cleared up and went to bed. We both had work in the morning."

"And that was the last time you saw Mr Prentice?"

"Yes. I've told you."

"How did he seem when he left?"

"Sorry?"

"Did he seemed worried, distracted?"

"No, he seemed his usual self."

"He didn't suggest that he stayed the night?"

"No." She shook her head. A frown creased her forehead.

"And neither you nor Mr Watkins left the house until you left for work the next morning?"

"Yes. Look, should I have a lawyer here? Am I under arrest?"

"No, you are just helping us with our inquiries for the moment. A number of things have come to light and we are trying to fill in some gaps. Now, would it be possible for Mr Watkins to leave the home without you knowing?"

"No. Why should he?"

"Are you sure he couldn't have slipped out after you had retired for the night?"

"No. Look I don't like this. I think I would like a lawyer here."

Inspector Greenwold stood. "Please take Miss Watkins to a phone, Sergeant, and then to a cell until her lawyer arrives."

While Katie was using the phone, Stephen was brought in and sat in the chair she had just vacated.

"Look, what is all this, Inspector? Why are we here?"

"You are here, sir, because four people are dead. Now that probably doesn't mean much to you but it does to us," he said sharply.

Stephen looked chastened. "I'm sorry. I didn't mean to imply…"

"Apology accepted, now can we get on?" Stephen looked shocked at the inspector's manner but saw no sympathy in Cotteril's face.

"Yes, of course. How can I help you?"

"Could you please go over the events of the night Mr Prentice was killed just one more time?"

"Well, he came round after work. We had a meal, Katie had cooked; it was her turn that night. We watched a little TV then Brian, sorry, Mr Prentice said he had to go as he had to be in a meeting first thing the next morning."

"And at what time was that?"

"I can't be precise but as the program hadn't quite finished I would say around ten to twelve."

"And he left alone?"

"Yes."

"You didn't walk part way with him?"

"No. Both Katie and I had to be up in the morning so we just said goodnight on the doorstep."

"And how did he seem to you?"

"Tired. He had had a gruelling day. He shouldn't have come round really but…" he tailed off. "He hadn't been very talkative and certainly didn't know what program we had been watching. His mind was elsewhere."

"And where would that be, sir?"

"Probably his kids. They're nothing but trouble. Spoilt rotten, both of them."

"Did they cause him much distress then?"

"Oh I'll say. That Scott was certain to get done for…" He stopped himself, realising what he was about to say.

"We know all about Master Prentice's habit, sir. Please continue."

"Well, yes. And then there's his daughter, the apple of his eye," he spat vehemently. "She thinks it's a hardship if she has to wait a week for the latest Prada handbag. Hasn't done a day's work in her life."

Cotteril could not be sure if Stephen was outraged because of his children's demands on Mr Prentice or if he was plain jealous.

"Your sister, sir."

"Yes?"

"I take it you're worried about her welfare as well?"

He snorted, "Naturally."

"And how long has she been seeing Scott?"

"Six months, I…" He looked up into the inspector's face. Greenwold leant forward and lowered his voice.

"And how long have you been seeing Brian?"

Stephen's mouth opened and shut a few times then he closed it and gave a resigned shrug. "Two years, well more like two and a half."

The inspector sat back, a satisfied look on his face. "Now that wasn't so difficult, was it, sir? If you had made us aware it was *you* he was seeing and not let us believe it was your sister, who knows? Maybe some lives would have been saved."

Stephen looked suitably downcast.

"I will be charging you with attempting to pervert the course of justice. I suggest you get in touch with your lawyer." And with that he stood and left the room, Cotteril in his wake.

As they walked down the corridor he held his hand up to silence Sergeant Cotteril.

"The photograph in Katie's room before you ask, also something I missed entirely, the photographs in the living room. Mr Prentice was always next to him, not Katie, except for just one of them. I wish I had realised sooner."

"What now then? You think it was Mrs Prentice because he was queer?"

Inspector Greenwold winced at the sergeant's coarseness. "I believe we are obliged to say he was "gay", Sergeant," he reprimanded.

"Sorry."

"And yes, I do think Mrs Prentice is involved although…" he stopped, walked, and gazed into middle distance. He shook his head, "there's something that still doesn't add up. Let's speak to the spoilt brats, shall we?"

Scott was draped over his chair. He had turned it sideways on so he could nonchalantly hang one arm over its back whilst rapping the fingertips of the other on the table. He hardly acknowledged the inspector and sergeant's entrance.

"Mr Prentice," Inspector Greenwold said to catch his attention. He looked round as if noticing them for the first time.

"At last someone intelligent," he said in a haughty manner. Somewhat different from when I last had words with him, Sergeant Cotteril thought to himself.

"Look, how long are you going to keep me here? I have things to do you know."

"Oh not long now," the inspector smiled. Cotteril had seen more sincere smiles on crocodiles at the zoo. "Then after you've been to court you'll be spending quite some time at another of Her Majesty's establishments. Or had you forgotten the fiasco with your drug supplier?"

Scott's face was a picture. An abstract, but a picture nonetheless.

"But… But surely..." he stuttered, his face reddening.

"You didn't think we would let that go, did you?"

"But…"

"We wouldn't be doing our job very well if we just turned a blind eye to every breach of the law, would we?"

Scott's attitude changed to one of defeat.

"Now, I want some answers and I want them straight. No bravado, no posing, just answers. Understand?"

"Yes."

"How long had you known you father was gay?"

If you had tipped a bucket of water over him you wouldn't not have got a more shocked reaction.

"What? I mean… How did…?"

"It's our job to find these things out. And you knew because you met the lovely Katie through your father's relationship with her brother, didn't you?"

He nodded dumbly.

"So, how long had you known?"

"About a year," he said quietly.

"And how long before you started blackmailing him?"

"Eh? What? Blackmail him because he's gay? Who would give a damn. Mother knew before I did, well, I suppose she would."

"No, not because he's gay, because you put two and two together and realised he had been extorting money from his company to pay for his love nest."

The reaction was as though a spike had been forced through the seat of his chair. "I don't…"

"How long?" the inspector interrupted his protestation, slamming his hand on the table.

He looked at his feet. "Not long."

"I'm sorry? I didn't quite hear that. Could you speak up for the tape please, Mr Prentice."

"I said, not long," he almost shouted.

"Thank you. So we can add that to the charge sheet. Now let's see if we can trump that with a murder charge."

"Now wait a minute!" he stood sharply and Cotteril jumped to his feet, ready for him. Scott decided he probably would come second in an altercation with the sergeant, but he leant over the desk to the inspector. "Now you look here…"

"*Sit down*." Both words were spat at him. He looked at the sergeant who still looked as if he was only just holding himself in check and sat again.

"What was it then? He called your bluff? He said 'go ahead' and in a fit of rage you killed him."

"No!"

"You knew he was due at Stephen's that night; all you had to do was hang around outside."

"No!"

"You waited until you were in the park then." The inspector thrust his arm at Scott, making him recoil in his chair. "Right up to the hilt." He sat back and studied the young man opposite him. "Perfect isn't it, Sergeant. Now that he can't wring any more money out using blackmail, he went for the mother-load. The inheritance."

"*No!*" he stood again, this time knocking his chair over and ignoring Sergeant Cotteril. "You've got it wrong. I don't get anything. Well," he corrected, "not much. Not as much as Stephen."

"I beg your pardon?"

"He changed his will. He left the bulk to Stephen. Mum gets the house and sis and I get fifty thousand each. It's Stephen you should be interrogating, he gets over half a million." He noticed he was shouting. He looked at the two men and sank to his seat. "It wasn't me."

Greenwold stood up, "Only because you hadn't thought of it," he said. "You have shown no remorse or grief since the day you were told. If being a heartless, ungrateful, selfish brat were a crime we would be throwing the key away with you."

"So, back to Stephen then, sir?" Cotteril asked as Scott was dragged away.

"No. Mr Prentice didn't register that will," he said, handing Cotteril a piece of paper from the file he had been carrying.

"Oh!"

"Yes, but first little Miss Prentice, I think. Let's see what she has to say for herself."

"Aren't these colours drab," she said, looking around the walls of the room. "Could I have a cup of tea please?" Then, as Cotteril stood, she said, "Darjeeling would be nice, thank you." She dismissed him as she would a servant.

"I'm sorry, we only have PG Tips here," the inspector said in a fatherly tone. "I'm afraid the police force doesn't provide a selection of teas."

"Oh! How terrible. You would think they would, wouldn't you." She studied her nails. She had decided he wasn't there for the moment.

This young woman, on the other hand, fascinated the inspector. She had cost her parents a small fortune and would contribute absolutely nothing to the gene pool. "Spare the rod and spoil the child," his dad used to say, and sitting across from him was a prime example.

He was shaken from his reverie by Cotteril entering the room with a tray and three cups of tea; one looked like cold dishwater. Cotteril handed this one to Geraldine.

"They didn't have Darjeeling, I hope Earl Grey will do?"

She graced him with a radiant smile and then scowled at the inspector.

Once they had all taken a drink from their cups and replaced them on the table, the inspector opened up the questioning.

"You're very close to your mother, aren't you?" he asked.

She smiled, "Yes. Mummy says we are more like sisters or bestest chums," she gushed.

"Do you do a lot together?"

"Oh yes. We go shopping up town every week together. That's when I'm not away on the continent of course." She looked thoughtful. "I don't know what she does then," she said.

"And you go away together, on holiday?"

"Oh yes," she laughed. "We have some *great* times on holiday."

"Where do you go?"

"Oh everywhere. New York, Italy, France, sometimes the Far East. We buy such lovely things. Clothes and jewellery and shoes, oh God the shoes in Italy, they're divine," she giggled happily.

"Did your father go with you too?"

"Daddy?" she said, askance. "Oh no. It's just me and Mummy." She smiled brightly at the men. "He goes skiing you know. In France. Scott has been with him a few times."

There was a knock at the door and DS McGuire beckoned for Greenwold to leave the room. Sergeant Cotteril terminated the interview on the tapes and followed. Geraldine was in a world of her own by time he had reached the door.

Inspector Greenwold was saying, "I hope this is to tell me you've found the suit."

"Sorry sir, no. But we have found something."

"Yes?"

"Forensics have them at the moment but there was a pair of black trainers in the bottom of one of the wardrobes, under a pile of other shoes. We think there may be traces of blood on them."

"What?" Greenwold's face broke into a broad grin. "Don't tell me we're going to finally find something for them to play with? I was beginning to think the killer was forensically trained." He rubbed his hands together. "I want to know the instant they find something. The instant, you hear?"

"Yes sir."

"Now get back down there and make a nuisance of yourself. I know you're good at that, McGuire, so don't let me down."

"Consider it done, sir," he grinned and trotted off to catch the lift before the doors closed. "Oi! Hold it a minute," he shouted.

"Right. Who's your money on then, Sergeant?"

"Mrs Prentice. I think McGuire's right."

"So do I, especially now we know there's another will somewhere. Mind you, I'll be amazed if we find it. I bet that got burned the second it was found.

"We have a motive, Sergeant. A big fat motive." He turned and walked back into the interview room.

Geraldine Prentice was as Cotteril had left her. Staring absently into space, her hands resting demurely on her crossed knees. She looked like one of those old paintings that hung in the portrait gallery in London.

"I'm sorry about the interruption, Miss Prentice, now if we could continue." She came back to the present and smiled at the inspector. "Now, you were saying about your holidays and that your father and brother went skiing together."

"Oh yes," she said, brightening now that she was the centre of attention again.

"Was it just the two of them or did they go in a group?"

"Oh there were two more who went with them. They always went together."

"I've never skied, I suppose it must be an addictive sport?"

"Oh I wouldn't know about that. I went once, it was beastly cold and I broke almost all of my fingernails on those stupid boot things. Why do they have to make them so hard to get on and off? And they rub. I was raw by the time we got home. No more for me, I said. And I never went again." She looked pleased with herself.

"Do you know the others who went?"

"Vaguely. There was a girl, Scott was sweet on her. And." She stopped abruptly, her faced clouded over with a scowl. "Can I go now?" she suddenly asked.

"Not just yet, miss. I would like to know more about these other people who went with your father skiing."

"Oh they're nobodies," she said dismissively.

"Wasn't your father seeing the young woman? The one you said Scott was sweet on?"

"No."

"We have reason to believe he was having an affair with her. Did you know she lives in Perry Green?"

"No. I mean, he wasn't, and yes I do know where she lives."

"He was paying for that flat she lived in. We traced it back to him."

Her eyes widened in outrage. "What? He was paying for that... that... queer!" she spat out.

"I'm sorry? I don't understand?" the inspector goaded.

A smug, superior expression settled on her face. "It wasn't the tart that Daddy was boofing. It was the queer. Her brother. Daddy was a queer."

"Boofing", Inspector Greenwold thought; that's a new one. "No, I think you've got that wrong. We found he was going to leave some money to her in his will. Quite a few thousand. So it must have been her."

She laughed. "You stupid man. It was him. Daddy was leaving it to him. And it wasn't a few thousand," she said sarcastically, "it was bloody everything." Now her face clouded over with anger. "Over half a bloody million he was leaving to that... that queer." She hit the table with her hand making the men jump. "And what about me? What would *I* get? A few lousy thousand, that's what. Wouldn't last a year."

"But they weren't mentioned in his will." The inspector banked on her being so enraged that she would not notice that it was he who first said about the inheritance.

"Not *that* will. Not the one before. A new will. I found it. It arrived in the post. I was expecting an invite to a weekend in the country and I opened it. I couldn't *believe* what I read. He'd virtually cut me out of his will. Me! His daughter! And for who? A bloody poof."

"That's not right," the inspector nudged.

"Bloody right it's not right," the accent was steadily sliding from upper class, through middle to where it should be. "How dare he? How bloody dare he? I'm his daughter. *I* should get it, not that…"

"So you had to stop it. It's only right," the inspector led her. "Did you try to talk to him?"

"*Him*? Why would I talk to him? Oh no, something had to be done, and it was."

"So you told your mother?"

"Later. Afterwards."

"Afterwards?"

"Yes. Afterwards. After I went to see that ponce of his. To tell him to get lost and to leave my father alone. I was going to tell him, he wasn't getting anything apart from a sore arse." Definitely working class now, the inspector thought. "I was so annoyed. I was soooo mad. I didn't care it was late at night, and there's all sorts in that park you know. I was going right round there and, and cut his cock off and shove it up his arse. That's what I was going to do."

"And did you?"

"Eh?" She seemed lost in the past for a moment but the inspector brought her back. "Oh, no! While I was walking across the park I saw Daddy coming the other way. He'd been to his boyfriend's. They'd been doing disgusting things to each other. He'd been in that pervert's bed and they'd been doing…" she looked as if she were about to explode. "So I stabbed him." She laughed. "You should've seen the look on his face." I did, the inspector thought. "He was so surprised. He didn't make a sound, he just fell. Well. That was that. No more will."

"And what did you do then? Did you go home or on to the flat?"

"Home. I went home. I… I didn't feel well. I went to bed."

"When did you tell your mother?"

"Mummy? Oh the next day. She was angry with me until I told her about the will and showed her it. Then she said I did the right thing. And I did, didn't I?" She looked for approval from the two men. She was wasting her time.

"I think that's enough. Miss Prentice I am arresting you for the murder of your father, Mr Brian Prentice. Read her her rights, Sergeant."

"What? You can't! I *had* to do it. Don't you see? He was giving my money away. He had to be stopped. Mummy said I had done the right thing. It *had* to be done, she said so. Where's Mummy, I want Mummy. What?"

The Sergeant and a WPC helped her to her feet.

"Where are you taking me? Can I go now? I told you everything. I've been good, can I go now?"

Her voice faded as she was led to the cells.

"Blimey!" Cotteril blew a gust of air through his cheeks. "What a head case."

"Sergeant!" Greenwold admonished. "I don't want her getting off on diminished, keep those remarks to yourself. Besides, she's been to university; she's travelled all over - and not always with 'Mummy'. She *has* got a brain in that head, it's just wired wrong.

"And now," Greenwold said, calming down, "for the mother. I think I'm going to enjoy this."

Chapter 29

Before interviewing Mrs Prentice, Inspector Greenwold checked in with the troops. The suit seen by Sergeant Cotteril was nowhere to be found. Even the local landfill site was being searched but for once millions of flies and thousands of seagulls were wrong, there was nothing of interest there.

"Anything from Forensics yet?" he asked the room. A general shaking of heads was the tired reply. "DNA?" he asked hopefully.

"Takes bloody weeks. They're too busy proving paternity to do mundane murder scene evidence," McGuire said in his usual laconic style.

"Couldn't we get it prioritised?"

A "you must be joking" expression painted itself on the seasoned detective's face.

"Forget I asked. So: no suit, no results from the lab and no chance of DNA this side of Christmas. Brilliant. A fine example of today's police force in inaction. I suppose we'll have to do it the old way. Get the rubber truncheons, Sergeant, we're going to interview the prime suspect."

Cotteril and Greenwold made their way back to the where Mrs Prentice was being kept on a low simmer.

She was sitting stiffly on the hard wooden chair in the interview room. If looks could kill she would have been on a genocide charge by the time the inspector and sergeant arrived.

"About bloody time. Where the hell have you been? And what have you done with Geraldine?" Her comments were noted and ignored as the sergeant went about the business of installing the evidence tapes in the recorder. Inspector Greenwold made the introductions on tape and the interview started.

"Mrs Prentice…"

"I said, where is Geraldine? What have you done with her? I want to see her. I demand…"

"*Mrs Prentice*," Inspector Greenwold repeated at a higher volume to stem her outburst. "The sooner you answer our questions, the sooner you get out of here." She seemed placated by his words and settled back in her chair. "Now, do you want your lawyer present?"

She looked from one deadpan face to the other. "Yes," she said, a worried expression now creasing her forehead.

Inspector Greenwold nodded to the sergeant who left the room and returned with Mrs Prentice's lawyer.

"Mr Ellis representing Mrs Prentice has now entered the room. Please be seated, sir."

The lawyer made a motion with his hand to quieten Mrs Prentice. "May I ask the nature of the charge that my client is being held under?"

"Mrs Prentice has not been charged with anything as yet. She is helping us with our inquiries into the spate of murders that have blighted Perry Green this last month or more."

"And how long has she been held here?"

"She hasn't been held at all. She came voluntarily and could leave at any juncture."

Mrs Prentice's head snapped round at that. "You mean I could have walked anytime I liked?" she asked incredulously.

"But of course."

"Why didn't you tell me?"

"A good question, I would say," the lawyer added.

"You were told on a number of occasions that you were not being charged with anything and were helping us with our inquiries."

"That doesn't answer my question."

"Doesn't it?" the inspector said, the image of innocence.

"I really must object," Mr Ellis interjected. "I think this charade has gone on long enough. Come, Mrs Prentice, let's…"

"Before you do that," the inspector said, opening a file in front of him and perusing it in the manner of a head teacher about to read out offences committed by a pupil before bestowing the cane on him, "I should inform you that your daughter, Miss Geraldine Prentice, has confessed to the killing of her father, Mr Brian Prentice, on the night in question and has made a full statement to that fact."

After a stunned few seconds Mrs Prentice exploded out of her chair, a lioness defending her cub. "You bastards! You tricked her. You forced it out of her. You put the words into her mouth," she raged.

The inspector just shook his head slowly. "On the contrary, Mrs Prentice, she gave it of her own free will. Seemed quite proud of the act."

"Are you going to just sit there?" she turned on her lawyer.

"I am here to defend you, Mrs Prentice. I was not privy to the interview of, Miss Prentice."

"Didn't you offer her a lawyer?" Mrs Prentice turned to the inspector.

"But of course, it's all in the transcript of the taped interview. It would be quite wrong of me not to, an infringement of her rights. I offered to call her lawyer several times but she declined."

Mrs Prentice was seething but controlling it with effort.

"I should warn you that she implicated you as an accessory after the fact Mrs Prentice. Hence this interview, to clear up any misunderstanding and to hear your side of things."

She looked lost, defiant but lost.

"When we first called on you, you said you were expecting your husband home that night and had gone to bed rather than wait up, is that so?"

"Yes."

"And yet, when you answered the door to us it was bolted on the inside. We distinctly heard you withdrawing the bolts and chain."

She looked dumbfounded.

"So, either you were not expecting him home that night or…" he paused dramatically, "someone else came home after you had gone to bed and locked up, knowing he wouldn't be home."

She just sat, her mind racing.

"Miss Prentice was that person, wasn't she?"

"No!"

"But you were expecting him home. You wouldn't have bolted the door, he wouldn't be able to get in."

"Um, I was teaching him a lesson. He was always out late seeing… seeing that…" Her lawyer leant across and whispered in her ear, silencing her.

"Yes?" the inspector asked.

She looked down at her hands in her lap saying nothing.

"When we told you what had happened, that was a genuine shock, wasn't it?

"It was later that you found out what had really happened. When your daughter told you. Tell me, did you know she was there when we arrived?"

"What? Oh, yes. Yes of course I knew she was there," she rallied.

"That's strange, isn't it, Sergeant?"

"Yes, sir," he obediently played his part in that well-known police double act called "Oh dear, oh dear, oh dear!"

"Because when we asked you, you said you were alone and the children, that is Scott and Geraldine, were at university. In fact, you told us Miss Prentice was abroad." He leant forward. "Are you sure you knew she was there?"

She didn't raise her head. She didn't make a sound, but Inspector Greenwold could plainly hear the cogs churning in her head.

"Mrs Prentice?" She looked up. "For the tape, Mrs Prentice," he asked.

She took a deep breath, having made up her mind. "Yes, I knew she was there. But she didn't kill him, I did. She must have bolted the door without my knowing."

"Why?" the inspector interrupted.

"Sorry?"

"Why did you kill him? Why didn't you just divorce him? Why bring all this on yourself when you don't have to? You seem an intelligent woman if I may say so, Mrs Prentice. I'm sure you could have divorced your husband and been able to lay claim to the lion's share of the proceeds if you put your mind to it. So, my question is: why?"

She sat with her mouth open. She couldn't think of a plausible answer.

He leant forward again. "You didn't kill him, did you?" he said.

"Then why…" the lawyer started to ask but was silenced by Greenwold's upheld hand.

"I am coming to that, Mr Ellis. But first I want to hear Mrs Prentice confirm that she did not, in fact, murder her husband."

She must have felt his eyes boring into the top of her head; she slowly looked up and shook her head, tears welling up in her eyes.

"Mrs Prentice shook her head indicating a negative answer," Cotteril said for the benefit of the tape.

"He drove her to it," she said in a small voice.

"I'm sorry?" the inspector prompted.

"I said, he drove her to it."

"How?"

She shook her head from side to side, getting her thoughts in order. "Gerri found a new will in his mail. It rescinded his previous will leaving the bulk of his estate to his boyfriend." She sneered as she spoke the last word. "That prancing rent-boy ensnared him." She looked up, stronger now. "He had a weakness, you see. I knew it before we married but I thought I would cure him. And I did, for a while. The children are not immaculate conceptions." Greenwold nodded encouragingly. "But then he met Stephen." She almost spat on the floor. "Blind man could see he was gay and that attracted Brian. You see, he couldn't control himself. So I turned a blind eye.

"At first I tried to win him back but he was smitten. That's when I decided we should have separate rooms. I didn't want him climbing into bed with me after he'd been with him and done all sorts of…" she sighed. "So we started living separate lives while all the time appearing to be the happy family."

"So what went wrong with the arrangement?" Although, the inspector was pretty sure he knew, he had to confirm his suspicions.

She gave a hollow laugh, "Scott happened. He had got in with the drug taking at uni and run up debts. He lied to us to start with to get money out of us, but it was never enough. Then he realised what was happening with his father and that… *person*, and threatened to go to the press or MacAllistair. Brian would have lost everything, and for what? A piece of arse."

Inspector Greenwold didn't bother to correct her. He didn't want to interrupt the flow.

"So, he paid him. His own son. He had to pay his own son to keep quiet about his … problem." She looked up. "Can you imagine what that did to our family? Can you imagine the scenes in our house? My God! I nearly went mad. All I had was Gerri so I poured all my attention and affection on her. She wasn't going to be dragged down by this. She would be kept out of it if it was the last thing I'd do."

"But it got out of hand?"

"Yes. Gerri discovered the will and … well I can only imagine she went berserk. She's such a gentle, loving child." Greenwold saw the knife sticking out of Prentice's chest and the expression on his face in his mind. Gentle and loving were not words that sprang to mind when describing his assailant. Driven, purposeful, cold - they were more like it.

"She told me that morning after your policewoman had left, I didn't even know she was there."

"What about the pizza?" Cotteril interjected and got a stern look from Greenwold for his trouble.

"Eh?"

"The pizza you had that night, there were two portions…" He stopped; she was staring at him coldly.

"We found a pizza box in your dustbin. It had the order taped to the lid and there were two…" Greenwold tried to explain, wishing Cotteril had not stepped in when he did.

"Oh *that!*" she said, catching on to what they were talking about. "What's that got to do with anything? I had ordered it for Brian and me. When he didn't show I put his on a plate in the oven in case he wanted it when he got in. Why? What do you want to know about that for?"

Another red herring, Greenwold thought ruefully to himself. We could stock an aquarium with the damn things. "So you hadn't ordered it for Geraldine and yourself?"

"No, Gerri wouldn't touch pizza, hates it. I didn't know she was there until I heard her upstairs and thought…" she paused, her eyes reddening again. "I thought it had all been a mistake and Brian was upstairs." Tears ran down her cheeks. "I ran to meet him, to tell him what I had been told and … and it was Gerri." Ellis handed her a handkerchief, she took it and wiped her eyes.

"She told me what she had done. I went mad. Then she told me why. Well, I couldn't have that. I couldn't have that queer tearing our family apart. Denying my daughter her rightful inheritance. So…"

"So you contrived to cover it up, didn't you?" the inspector said.

She nodded. "We are the same size, you see. I made her show me the clothes she wore. I was sure they would be covered in blood but they weren't. I made her show me how she had done it then I sent her back to uni and…"

"And you thought if there were enough bodies, we may lose sight of this one."

She nodded again, Sergeant Cotteril told the tape.

There was a cautious knock at the door, Cotteril got up and answered it.

"Sergeant Cotteril has left the room," Greenwold said for the tape. "Go on."

"Well I destroyed the will. Burned it. Then… Then I used Gerri's clothes, except the shoes. Her feet are quite dainty compared to mine." She looked up as Cotteril re-entered the room. Greenwold told the tape. He whispered in his superior's ear, who nodded and then they looked to Mrs Prentice to continue.

"I had to do it," she pleaded. "I had no choice. I had to protect my little girl."

"And the others. The people you used to cover up your husband's death?"

"I didn't know them," she said in a matter-of-fact way. "They were just… people."

"One was a young girl."

"A nobody. A council estate girl. What was she compared to my Gerri, I ask you. Nothing."

"The policeman?"

"Pardon?"

"The policeman. Well, a specialist actually, but he was working for us."

"Who was?"

"The man outside the pub."

"Him? He was helping you?" she looked genuinely amazed. "I had no idea. He was just some old drunk coming out of that pub.

"And Mr Quinn? The man in the garages?"

"Oh *him*!" she said with bile. "He was disgusting. I saw him, you know, with her. That little tubby tart. He was shagging her in the back of his car. It was rocking about all over the place. I waited and thought, why not? Why not kill this silly little tart. But a car came by and I had to hide and by the time I came back she had gone and there was just him."

"So you killed him instead?"

"Yes, I had to. You do understand, don't you? I had to protect my…" Her pleading eyes met only hard, judgemental stares. Then the enormity of it all hit her like a truckload of bricks and her head fell to the table sobbing.

Epilogue

"A job well done." It was the superintendent who was heaping praise on the reluctant heads of Inspector Greenwold and Sergeant Cotteril. "So the girl killed her father and the mother killed all the others to cover it up. Brilliant. Had us on a wild goose chase, that's for sure."

"I'm glad it amuses you, sir." Greenwold said.

The super looked hurt. "What's the matter with you, man? You solved it. Pity there's no forensic to tie it up."

"Oh but there is," Cotteril butted in. "The trainers. They had Mr Quinn's blood on them."

"And they are definitely the mother's?"

"Yes sir. She takes two sizes larger than her daughter and we found the receipt in her handbag for them. Dated the day after Mr Prentice's death. There's sure to be her DNA on them to put it beyond doubt."

"So, that's that then," he said. "Cheer up, Joe. It's a good collar as they say on telly. What's eating you, man?"

"Doctor Ransom."

"Oh!"

"I sent him to that pub. Recommended it. Because of me..."

"No!" the super butted into Greenwold's guilt trip. "*Not* because of you. It was because of *her*. A man, or woman for that matter, should be able to go for a drink without getting a kitchen knife rammed into their chest. It was *her* fault, no one else's, d'you hear?"

"Yes sir."

"Don't you 'yes sir' me in that tone of voice. Sergeant, I order you to take him to the pub and pour beer down him until he either passes out or sees sense."

"Yes sir."

In the pub, the same pub that Ransom had had his last drink in, Greenwold and Cotteril along with McGuire, Mills, Chatris and some of the others, drank as only coppers could. They drank to forget, to purge their memories of what they had had to witness. The atrocities that man inflicted on fellow man, or in this case, that woman inflicted on man.

"They lose touch with reality," Greenwold said to no one in particular. Everyone was talking but no one was listening, it was that late in the day. "When they get wealth, they get … I dunno, remote from the real world.

"It's not like they had masses of money. Not like rock stars or politicians or royalty. They were just comfortably off and that's what they'd descended to."

He tried to take another draught from his empty glass and stared at it when it didn't deliver. He put it down and Cotteril snatched it up to refill it, orders were orders after all.

"You know, when William Golding wrote *Lord of the Flies*, he should have used middle class couples instead of children. Then you would have seen some… some… stuff, atrocity… atroc… Where's my drink gone? Oh ta." He looked at Cotteril and stopped him raising a glass to his lips. "Oh no you don't. You're driving me home. I don't want to have to breathalyse you." Then he burst out laughing at Cotteril's wounded expression. The rest of the crowd joined in, but they didn't really know or care why. It was just good to laugh.

The End